VENGEANCE

Center Point
Large Print

Also by Wade Everett and available from Center Point Large Print:

Texas Ranger
Bullets for the Doctor

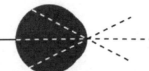

**This Large Print Book carries the
Seal of Approval of N.A.V.H.**

VENGEANCE

Wade Everett

CENTER POINT LARGE PRINT
THORNDIKE, MAINE

This Center Point Large Print edition
is published in the year 2015 by arrangement with
Golden West Literary Agency.

First US edition: Ballantine Books.
First UK edition: Collins.

The text of this Large Print edition is unabridged.
In other aspects, this book may vary
from the original edition.
Printed in the United States of America
on permanent paper.
Set in 16-point Times New Roman type.

ISBN: 978-1-62899-773-6 (hardcover)
ISBN: 978-1-62899-778-1 (paperback)

Library of Congress Cataloging-in-Publication Data

Everett, Wade.
 Vengeance / Wade Everett. — Center Point Large Print edition.
 pages cm
 Summary: "Dan Colley was a reformed gunfighter, turned rancher. But
trouble wouldn't leave him alone because Dan was not the kind of man
to sit idly by while a neighbor was in danger of his life from a cattle
king too big for his boots"—Provided by publisher.
 ISBN 978-1-62899-773-6 (hardcover : alk. paper)
 ISBN 978-1-62899-778-1 (pbk. : alk. paper)
 1. Large type books. I. Title.
 PS3553.O5547V46 2015
 813′.54—dc23
                                                           2015032429

VENGEANCE

1

Dan Colley was just sitting down to supper when Al Ritchie rode into the yard and tied up. He clomped across the porch because he was a big man who never pretended to be delicate, and he opened the back screen door without knocking. Edith Colley looked around, her round face showing her disapproval, but Ritchie ignored her.

He had a shotgun cradled in the crook of his arm and a coil of rope draped over one shoulder. "I thought I was going to meet you at the fork?" Ritchie said.

"I've changed my mind, Al," Colley told him. "I'm going to stay out of it." He was a young man, barely twenty-five. The land was his because his father had left it to him, and people were already saying that it was too much for him to handle. Colley had a face that most men would have a hard time remembering because he had no prominent features that stuck in a man's mind. His hair was brown, just brown, and his eyes had no particular hardness or steadiness; they were not the eyes of a man who controlled nearly eleven thousand acres of mortgage-free land. "Why don't you leave it to the sheriff, Al?"

"He's out of the county," Al Ritchie said. "He's not going to do anything, anyway."

Edith Colley said, "Al, this is none of your business. It wasn't your steer. Why do you have to poke your nose into other people's business?"

He stared at her, for she was one of those farmer girls from up valley who had married into cattle, and somehow he would never be able to understand this, or excuse her. But he had too much sense to show this feeling to Dan Colley. He smiled and said, "Edith, it's man's business, and if we're ever goin' to have law and order, then we've got to make it ourselves."

"By taking a man out of jail and lynching him?" she snapped. "I suppose the rope is to tie your horse?" She was young, hardly more than nineteen, but she had fight in her; a man could tell that at a glance, and Dan Colley knew it, for he reached out and patted her hand. She fell silent, then got up and went to the stove for the coffeepot. She moved carefully, for she was swollen with child.

Al Ritchie said, "Hell, Dan, you ought to come along anyway, just to make sure some of the hotheads don't do anything foolish. You can leave any time you please, you know."

Edith poured Dan's coffee and said, "Go if you want to."

"I don't want to," he said. "But I don't want to see a mistake made, either."

"It was a mistake ever talking about it," she said, and looked at Al Ritchie. "Did you start it?"

He showed surprise and pointed to himself. "Me? Listen, I never lynched anyone."

"What's the rope for then?"

"It's a catch rope I'm taking to Waggoner! Hell, can't a man carry a rope anymore?" Then he laughed. "Finish your coffee, Dan. I'll catch up and saddle your horse." He went out then, slamming the screen door, scattering a swarm of flies that clung stubbornly to the screen.

Colley added sugar to his coffee and stirred it. "That damned sheriff is always off some place."

"With four counties to handle, what do you expect?" Edith said, her voice testy. Then she smiled. "Dan, surely there are enough men in town to stop this. Do what you can."

"That's what I intended to do. I'd like to count on Al, but he keeps riding the fence, and you never know which way he'll jump." He drank his coffee and put the cup aside. "A man ought to have a trial, no matter what." He got up and kissed her. "I'll be home before morning. You keep the door barred. I'll whistle when I come in the yard."

"Nothing's going to hurt me, Dan."

He laughed without humor. "That's what Swigley thinks, and he's sitting behind bars in a locked jail." He went into the bedroom for his coat because these nights turned cold toward morning. Outside they could hear Ritchie swearing at

9

Colley's horse; he did everything with a lot of trouble and fuss, even saddling up.

Dan Colley left his pistol hanging on the peg by the door, and Edith said, "Aren't you going to take that along?"

He shook his head. "A man may be better off without it tonight." He kissed her again, and he seemed apologetic about going, but she gave him a shove. He went outside, meeting Ritchie, who was leading the roan from the barn.

As they mounted, Ritchie said, "We'll meet Doe Stoddard at the crossroad. He's bringing Sam Mitchell along."

"You're expecting a crowd," Colley said, and turned out of the yard.

His place lay in a long valley, bracketed on both sides by mountains. They were big mountains, but dwarfed by the snow-covered peaks to the west; even in August they had a mantle on them, and he suspected that there were places up there where the snow never melted at all.

This was, he figured, the best country he had ever seen, and he had been Texas born and bred. But his father, after the war, had taken up land in this valley and named his brand after the mountains, the Wind River Range. Now WR was burned into the flanks of nearly three thousand head, and the father was dead. It was all Dan Colley's now, and he worked it with more knowledge and enthusiasm than anyone

10

had ever given him credit for or thought he had.

As he rode along, he supposed that he had made a pretty wild showing some years back. Before he left Texas, he had been in some trouble; he'd been fifteen then, and he'd shot a Yankee carpetbagger. Nothing serious, for the Yankee recovered and went back North, but it convinced some people that Dan Colley was going to be a wild one.

Wyoming in the late '60s was a wild place— no law, no courts—and if a man couldn't take care of himself, he soon got killed. The country suited Dan Colley to a T, and by the time he was eighteen, he'd already downed his man in a brand dispute, and his reputation started to grow.

But it was 1876 now, and he was older, two years married, three years sole owner of the WR spread. He wasn't sure what had calmed him down, but he didn't care whether or not he wore a gun, and he sincerely hoped that he would never have to use one again. Perhaps Edith had changed his philosophy, or maybe he changed it himself because the law was taking over and towns were growing and there were courts and judges—not many, and some not very good, but it was the right way.

And then he could look at Al Ritchie, just a few years older, but a man who had never changed at all. He still believed that you hung a thief, shot your man if you had to, and then told the sheriff just to get it on the record.

"You're not sayin' much," Ritchie broke in.

"I was thinking about you," Colley admitted. "Al, you're a wild bastard. Why don't you slow down?"

"What for? I like things the way they are."

"What do you want to do in town?"

Ritchie shrugged "Whatever the others want to do. As long as it's excitin'." He turned his head and peered at Dan Colley through the gathering dusk. "Shit, you're not afraid of hangin' a man, are you? There was a time when—"

"That time's done and gone," Colley said quickly. He pointed ahead where the road cut through a batch of timber; two men waited there, sitting their horses.

"Stoddard and Mitchell," Ritchie said. "We're late because you had to gab."

"Ride on if you're in a hurry," Colley suggested.

"We'll go in together," Ritchie stated.

Doe Stoddard was an older man, in his fifties, tall and grave, a man who complained constantly about everything changing, and liking none of it. He said, "Don't either of you own a damned watch?"

"We haven't been here long, Doe," Sam Mitchell cut in. He was a round man, as stout as a barrel, and inclined to be easygoing. He turned his horse and sided Dan Colley. "Have a little trouble makin' up your mind?"

"Some," Colley admitted.

"I was hopin' you'd come. That makes two of us, anyway." He nodded toward Stoddard and Al Ritchie, who rode ahead. "Al will be all right as long as he's runnin' things, and Doe will go along with anything if he thinks someone else will take the responsibility. I don't want to see anything happen to Swigley."

"Then don't let it," Colley said.

"What's all this fuss Al's makin', anyway?" Mitchell wanted to know. "Hell, it was your calf, wasn't it?" He turned and peered at Colley in the last of the remaining light. "Where the hell's your gun?"

"Am I going to need one?" Colley asked.

"Damn, if you do, you'll be in one hell of a fix."

They rode for a good hour and a half before they reached town. They all called it a town, but it was a settlement—a trading post, a few stores, a stable and blacksmith shop, and a way station that was infrequently touched by stages that had to venture north from Rawlins, the only town of size within a radius of one hundred miles, and Rawlins was closer to two hundred miles to the southeast.

While Cheyenne and Sun Dance and Douglas boomed, this section of the country stood aloof and remote, protected by giant mountains and brutal winters and roaring mountain streams that were always impassable in the spring and risky to cross any other time. It was a raw, new land, with perhaps no more than a few hundred people populating ten thousand square miles of it, and there seemed to be no tendency for people to rush in and crowd them.

All stores and freight came from Cheyenne and Rawlins, and from Rawlins it was hauled by ox freight because mules just didn't have the strength to handle heavy wagons in such mountainous country. And because of this, there were very few frills. Window glass was still an item that only the well-to-do and the patient could afford, because glass sold for three dollars a square foot, and you waited four months for it and hoped that half of it didn't arrive broken.

All the buildings were log, chinked with clay and moss and roofed with earth. These were common building materials, and the poor man used them as well as the ranchers like Colley and Ritchie and Stoddard. A man's station in life was marked only by the way the inside of the house was finished, for only a man showing a good profit could have his furniture hauled in from Laramie.

There were a half dozen horses tied in front of the trading post and farther down a cluster of wagons, for the farmers had come in, too. Al Ritchie found a place to tie his horse, and the others dismounted, tied up, and gathered in front of the store.

Then Ritchie said, "A drink sounds about right

to me," and went on in, with Doe Stoddard following at his heels.

Mitchell hesitated, and Dan Colley said, "You go on in. I'll go on over to the express office and see what's going on." He gave Mitchell a gentle shove. "Go on. Nothing's going to start now, anyway."

He turned and crossed the dark street and approached the express office, a squat log building jammed between the stage station hotel and a harness shop. Four farmers stood near the door, and Ed Gruen was there, his badge reflecting lantern light that seeped through the front window.

When Colley came up, Gruen straightened a little, as though he were getting ready for something and didn't know just what. "If there's trouble tonight, I'll shoot, Colley," Gruen said.

"If there's trouble, I want you to shoot," Colley told him. Then he looked at the farmers, and they watched him carefully, wanting to trust him because he'd married a farm girl, yet not trusting him because he was cattle and therefore a natural enemy.

One of them said, "Colley, what the hell's Ritchie after, anyway?"

"He's just shooting off his mouth," Colley said dryly. "He's always been a great talker."

"Talk gets people stirred up," another said.

Colley looked at Ed Gruen. "When's the sheriff due back?"

"Damned if I know. There was that shooting up in Buffalo—a couple of soldiers got into it with a card player." He shrugged. "He'll be back. I guess a judge is coming in from Cheyenne on the stage day after tomorrow."

One of the farmers said, "So Ritchie's got to move if he's going to, ain't he, Colley? He can't wait much longer."

"Listen," Colley said, "that was just talk. Ritchie's not going to lynch anyone, understand?"

A horseman came into town, and they looked toward the west end of the street; then Joe Waggoner dismounted by the trading post and tied up. He was a tall man who chewed tobacco constantly and said very little, but he was a man most everyone walked clear of, for he was always well armed and had an inclination to settle his arguments by shooting the opposition, always cleverly arranging it so that it was self-defense.

Waggoner ducked under the hitch rail, then stopped and peered across the street. "Colley? Ain't you on the wrong side?" He laughed and went inside, and an uneasy silence settled over the farmers standing by the express office.

"I'd feel better if we had a real jail," one said. "Something made of brick with bars on the windows."

"That wouldn't stop Ritchie," Ed Gruen said matter-of-factly. He carried a repeating Spencer rifle in the crook of his arm, and he shifted it to the other side. "Colley, you knew that Swigley got the calf. How come you didn't have him arrested?"

"Swigley was on his uppers. I don't let any man starve. He'd have asked me if I'd been around, but I was up Owl Creek way, two days' ride."

"It wasn't none of Ritchie's business," one farmer said. "He was just trying to make himself big."

"You're wrong there," Colley said. "If a man stole from you and I saw it, I'd report it. You can't expect a man to take care of himself all the time. The world's too big." He took out a sack of tobacco and rolled a cigarette. "I'm going across and see what's going on. Don't worry too much, Ed. Sam Mitchell thinks like I do."

"That's just two. Would you stand up to Joe Waggoner?"

"If I had to," Colley said gravely. "I wouldn't like to, not because he's slick with a six-shooter, but because I think there's other ways of handling a man besides killing him."

"Mitchell wouldn't face Waggoner," Gruen said. "He'll take any side that's safe."

"There's more to Sam than that," Colley said. He looked at the farmers and noticed that they were unarmed. "If you've brought shotguns, keep them in the wagons. The last thing we need is for someone to start shooting. You won't stop it if that happens."

"I'll shoot if I have to," Ed Gruen repeated.

"Sure, but you're a sworn officer of the law."

Gruen laughed. "Do you think Ritchie or Waggoner have any respect for the law?"

Dan Colley sighed. "No, unfortunately. Not a damned bit. But they've got to be taught."

"By who?" Gruen asked, and Colley didn't answer that; he turned and walked across the rutted street to the trading post.

2

Dunfee's saloon and trading post was the oldest building in the entire valley, for it had been built to serve the mountain men and fur trappers and to do business with the Indians. It was log, large, with an upper story that now served as a supply house; it had been built as a platform to fire rifles from in the event of attack. Dunfee's had been attacked many times, but had never fallen.

Dunfee was an old man, certainly over seventy, and he dispensed whiskey and trade goods from behind the hewn plank counters, and if someone got wild in his place, he still had the strength to dispense trouble. Early in his life—no one knew when—Dunfee had picked up a friend, Louis Bergerac, a runt of a man with an unkempt beard and a wildness in his eyes. They worked together, and it didn't really matter which was the boss, for they argued incessantly.

Ritchie was already at the bar, his friends lined up beside him, and when Dan Colley came in, they all turned their heads and looked. Then Ritchie had Dunfee bring another drink. Everything was served in tin cups, for glasses were too easily broken during the long distance from Laramie.

"How's your friend across the street?" Ritchie asked. Joe Waggoner, who was standing on the other side of Ritchie, laughed, and Dan Colley stared at him.

"What do you think's so funny?"

"The way you people waste time," Waggoner said. The rope that Ritchie had brought to town was now draped over Waggoner's shoulder. "If it was my doing, I'd have Swigley out of that jail and hung."

"It's not your doing," Sam Mitchell said, and Waggoner turned around.

"Would you stop me?" He waited for his answer and didn't get one, then he turned his head and looked at Dan Colley. "You would, though, wouldn't you? Have to get a gun, though. I wouldn't stop easy."

Louis Bergerac had been carrying boxes from the back room, opening them and putting goods on the shelf. Suddenly he'd had enough of this work and decided to sweep; he took up a broom and began to pile sawdust where they were all standing, forcing them back from the bar. None liked the interruption, yet none knew how to handle Bergerac; he was a wild old man who dressed like an Indian and had been known to display a mean streak.

Finally he swept his way near Dan Colley and said, "Got a wolf pelt I want you to see." He quickly put the broom aside and took Colley by the sleeve, dragging him into the back of the store.

Colley shook loose after they were out of the main room and said, "Damn it, what the hell you doin'?"

"Don't get het up," Bergerac said. "Can't you see Waggoner and Ritchie are fixin' to howl tonight? I heard that all of Ritchie's crew was comin' in tonight. Waggoner's, too. That mean anything to you now?"

"A bustout?"

"Hell, yes, what else? You want to see that sodbuster hung?"

"Not this way," Colley said.

"Then let's get to him before Ritchie does."

Colley laughed. "You want me to bust him out?"

"I'll help you. He'd be safer at your place, wouldn't he? Hell, you and I both know that Ed Gruen would think twice before he shot anyone. Waggoner knows that. So does Ritchie. Gruen might surrender him to you."

"You don't believe that," Colley said. "Gruen thinks he's the best deputy there ever was. We'd have to take Swigley away from him. And that's against the law."

"Law your ass! It's either you take him or Ritchie!"

Dan Colley wiped a hand across his mouth and had to admit that Bergerac had a point that couldn't be ignored. Ritchie was buying the drinks, and Waggoner had the rope, and it was all a bad combination. He said, "Meet me in front of the express office in fifteen minutes."

"Will do," Bergerac said, and Colley went back into the main room.

Mitchell said, "Did he get a wolf?"

"Just an old man's talk," Colley said, and lifted his cup and drained it. Ritchie started to pour another, but Colley put out his hand and covered the cup; this offended Ritchie but he did nothing about it, although Colley knew that he'd remember it. "I'm going out front for a spell," Colley said. "You've got drinking to do, and I don't feel like it, and when a man gets that way, he only spoils it for someone else."

He went out then and stood on the porch a few minutes, and then he heard Waggoner's heavy step as far as the door, checking on him. When Waggoner was satisfied, he went back to the bar. Then Dan Colley hurried across to the other side.

Bergerac and the farmers were there, and Bergerac turned as Colley came up. "He don't believe what I say, Dan."

"Told you he wouldn't," Colley murmured. He looked at Ed Gruen, then before the man knew what had happened, Colley hit him, flush on the jaw, and Bergerac caught him before he could fall. To the farmers, Colley said, "Gather close. Block our view across the street."

"Got the keys," Bergerac said, jangling them; he inserted one in the door, hit it lucky, and opened the front door.

To the farmers, Colley said, "I'll take him to my place. Not even Waggoner would be stupid enough to ride after him there, not with my crew. One of you fetch my horse around behind the building and be quiet about it."

He stepped inside then and went into the rear room where Bergerac was unlocking the door. Swigley backed into a corner, thinking that they were coming to lynch him, and he struck out as Bergerac reached for him.

There was little gentleness in the old Frenchman; he cuffed Swigley twice and said, "I got no time to jaw. Colley's takin' you to his place or you won't live to morning. Make a sound now and you're a gone beaver."

His manner, the tone of his voice convinced Swigley, and he nodded, and they all went out the back way. Bergerac had a horse waiting there for

Swigley, and a farmer came around with Dan Colley's. They mounted up and moved carefully to the end of the alley, then rode on out of town.

After they had gone a mile, Colley slowed, and Swigley said, "I've been scared this night, Mr. Colley."

"You're going to be scared other nights, too," Colley said. "Want some tobacco?" Swigley shook his head. "Let's ride then. It won't be long before Ritchie and Waggoner find out they've been tricked."

Swigley wanted to stay and talk, to thank Colley for taking him out of that locked room; Swigley could not understand that he was a long way from being safe. Even if he'd had a hundred-mile start, he would not have been safe, for this was wild country, and the kind of law that Waggoner and Ritchie stood for could reach a hundred miles and then some.

It was quite late when Colley reached his own ranch, and when he and Swigley rode into the yard, two men came out of the bunkhouse, one with a lantern and the other with a rifle.

Colley said, "This is Swigley, Scotty. Bergerac and I broke him out. Ritchie was buying the drinks, and Waggoner was beginning to talk brag."

The foreman said, "Did you have to bring him here?"

"You'd rather seen him strung up in the stable?"

He dismounted, and Swigley did the same, and the man with the lantern took the horses to the barn. "Go on in the house, Swigley. And don't stomp around and wake my wife." He watched the man walk away, then he took Scotty by the arm. "I don't think Waggoner will be fool enough to come here."

"If he's drunk enough, he would," Scotty said. "I'll wake a couple of the fellas who've been getting too much sleep lately, and we'll watch until dawn." He laughed. "You know, I hear Swigley wasn't much of a farmer, either."

"What does it matter what he was?" Colley asked, and walked on toward the house. Swigley was in the kitchen, stoking the fire to make some coffee, and he was pretty noisy about it, because he was a man who had trouble believing anything anyone else ever said.

"Damn it, I told you to be quiet, Swigley," Colley said, and took the poker away from him. But it was too late because Edith was already stirring; he heard her on the steps, and a moment later she came into the kitchen, blinking against the lamplight. She saw Swigley, then said, "Take your hat off in the house, Ike. You never did have a bit of manners."

Colley had the fire going, and Edith dippered the coffeepot full and put it right over the fire, taking a lid off the stove in order to set the coffeepot down. Then she looked at her husband.

"Al Ritchie wasn't going to do anything, huh?"

"Well, I don't know, because I never gave him a chance. But it sounded like trouble."

"Who helped you? Mitchell?"

Dan Colley shook his head. "Bergerac." He turned around and looked at Ike Swigley. "What the hell am I going to do with you? First you steal a calf and get caught, then I've got to break you out to keep you from being lynched."

"I didn't mean to make trouble, Mr. Colley. My family was hungry."

"Did you ever hear of work? Hell, if you'd asked, I'd have given you the beef."

"A man has his pride," Swigley said.

"A man can also be stupid. And that's you," Colley said.

Scotty knocked at the back door, then came in. "Dan, I've picked out two good horses and a pack horse. With any luck you can have him in Laramie in four days."

"What makes you think I'll take him to Laramie?" Colley asked.

"There's no other place. You don't want Waggoner to come here. And he would if he had Ritchie and the others to back him up. You want I should have the cook pack a couple sacks?"

Dan Colley sighed. "Sure, what the hell. I don't want a standoff here. Or even the threat of one."

"I can't ride to Laramie," Ike Swigley said.

"Mr. Colley, I'm not a good rider, and we'd have to travel fast, and—"

"Why don't you shut up?" Colley asked. The coffeepot bumped and rocked, and he took it off the fire while Edith got the cups and put them on the table. He filled them and added sugar to his, then sipped it very slowly. "The only chance of keeping you alive is to get you to Laramie and have your trial there, Swigley. I broke you out, and that's against the law. If you want to take your chances here, then I'll give you a horse and you can run for it. But Ritchie and Waggoner know this country, and they can track a cat across a flat rock, so you wouldn't get far. With me you'd stand a chance of making Laramie alive. Now what's it going to be?"

"There's no choice at all," Swigley whined.

"That's right," Colley said. "There wasn't any from the moment you butchered my beef." He glanced at Edith. "I'll take my pistol and rifle. See that the shell belt's full and that there's a box of rifle shells. I ought to be back in eight or nine days." Then he smiled and went around the table and put his arm around her. "I'm sorry, hon, but I just couldn't stand by and do nothing."

"I know. And I'd have wondered about you if you had," she said. "I'll get your gun." Her glance went to Swigley. "One for him, too?"

"The shotgun," Colley said. "You can use a shotgun, can't you?"

26

Swigley nodded. "What of my family?"

Colley said, "Well, what of them?"

"Who'll take care of them? My oldest is only nine."

"Who'd have done it after they lynched you? Man, can't you figure anything out for yourself?" Scotty came to the door and signaled that the horses were ready. "Drink your coffee and wait outside, Swigley. I'll be along in a minute."

He went into the bedroom then and picked up his pistol belt and buckled it around his waist. Edith was getting the rifle shells, and he dropped them into his coat pocket. He changed into another pair of pants and boots, rolled a spare shirt, and picked up saddlebag and rifle and took them outside and gave them to Scotty.

Edith was in the parlor when he went back in; he put his arms around her and kissed her and said, "I'll be back in nine days at the latest. If you begin to feel poorly, have Scotty take you into town. But don't wait until the last minute. If you want, Scotty can fetch the doctor here."

"That would be better," she said. "Dan, would it be all right if I sent someone over with a few things for Swigley's family?"

"Sure, do what you want." He kissed her again. "Now don't worry about what's going to happen. If Ritchie and Waggoner show up, they'll howl and stamp their feet, but they'll let it go at that. I'm sure Ritchie won't carry it further."

"And Joe Waggoner?"

Dan Colley shrugged. "He may follow me if he's drunk enough. Then he'll sober up and turn back. There's nothing in it for him. He just does what Al Ritchie says." He kissed her again and went out and stepped into the saddle because Swigley was already up and waiting, in a hurry now to get going.

"There's a good five hours until dawn," Scotty said. "You can make a lot of that, Dan. Good luck. And, farmer, for Christ's sake keep your knife out of other people's beef." He stepped back so that Colley could turn his horse, and they left the yard, the pack horse following on a long rope.

They rode east by southeast, moving steadily along the broad sweep of the valley, for dawn would bring them to the end of it and into a low range of mountains, and Colley was counting on making the high country by sunup. He was leaving a broad trail down the valley, but that couldn't be helped; it was only when he got into the rocky land and the game trails that he could travel and leave no sign that could be followed easily.

It wasn't possible for a man to travel with three shod horses and leave no sign at all, but a good man could clutter and confuse it and make the man trailing slow down and work carefully and thereby lose ground.

And a herd of elk, moving down toward evening graze and water, could blot out very effectively the trail left by three horses.

Dawn, the first gray flush of it, caught them climbing, and this pleased Colley, for they were making good time, although Swigley was tired and would cause trouble later. They kept climbing until the sun rose high enough to brighten the valley floor, then Colley stopped, got out his field glasses, and had a long careful look at the back trail.

Swigley said, "We aren't being followed, are we?"

"Don't bet on it," Colley told him, and put the glasses away.

"Did you see anyone?"

"Nope."

"Then we're not being followed."

Dan Colley laughed. "Mister, Waggoner's back there someplace. He's got to be because he's always said how good he is, and he's been looking for a chance to prove it."

"Good at what?"

"Man-catchin'," Dan Colley said, and then rode on.

3

It was only a question of time, a question of miles traveled and hours in the saddle before Ike Swigley began to play out, and when a man did that, he was going to make mistakes.

Swigley began to grumble about not stopping often enough; his rear end was sore because he was not accustomed to riding, and his pants had creased over and eaten him raw. Dan Colley knew how tough it was, but he couldn't stop because Waggoner was back there somewhere, following and working hard to catch up.

But they had to stop and rest the horses, and when they were ready to go on again, Swigley didn't want to mount up. Colley hit him once and bloodied his nose, and then Swigley got the idea that Colley meant it and went into the saddle, groaning because it tore his aching muscles and aggravated the bleeding places on his buttocks and thighs.

Swigley didn't want cold rations. He wanted hot coffee and a pan of bacon and some thick hotcakes, for he was sure that the fire would give off no smoke, and he could not be convinced that cooking odors linger long on the air.

At midday they settled for meat and bread and a swig from the canteen, not stopping more than fifteen minutes. Colley felt that it was important to cross the Sweetwater before nightfall, and he thought he could do it if he could keep Swigley going.

The man was clinging to the saddlehorn to stay mounted, and he rode with his eyes closed, letting Colley lead the horse, and although he hated to admit it, Colley knew that Swigley just didn't have it in him to make a dash like this, not to as faraway a place as Laramie. They'd have to stop, make camp, and make a stand of it because there wasn't any other way.

Alone, Colley knew that he could outrun Waggoner, cover his trail so well that Waggoner could never catch him, but Swigley just wasn't up to it.

The southeast bank of the Sweetwater would be the place, for there was a thick grove of trees on that shore near the crossing and Waggoner would look there first.

And I'll let him look, Colley thought, and kept on moving.

He had to keep on hiding his trail, for if he stopped doing that, it would plainly tell Waggoner that he was waiting up ahead. So Colley stayed to the rocky ground as much as he could, and as the sun started to slide down out of sight, they reached the Sweetwater. The current was not swift at that time of the year, and the horses balked a little, but he edged them in. Then when they went into the deep part and started swimming, he left the saddle and swam alongside, one hand gripping the pommel.

Swigley did a lot of splashing and nearly drowned before they reached the other shore, and Colley had to pull him from the water, and he rolled the man belly down across a deadfall to get the water out of him.

"We'll camp out there," Colley said finally, pointing to a stretch of open country.

"What's the matter with the grove?" Swigley asked.

"Open's better. Can you walk now?"

"Yeah, but I sure as hell can't ride another foot. My ass is raw."

"You've done all right, Swigley," Colley said. The man hadn't, really, but it didn't hurt anything to lie a little, and it made Swigley feel a whole lot better; he brightened and forgot his aches and raw places.

"I tried, Mr. Colley. Damned if I didn't." He chuckled. "I'm a little proud of myself at that." He turned in a circle. "You want me to fetch some wood for the fire?"

"Cold camp," Colley said. "We'll have company before morning."

He walked a hundred yards into the clear and stopped; Swigley had followed, and he didn't think much of the place, for there was no cover except the grass.

"Campin' out in the open like this don't make sense to me, Mr. Colley."

"Well, if Waggoner comes up, it'll be on his belly," Colley told him, and picketed the horses. "Tell you what—we'll eat, then I'll pick a spot for you. Once you're there, don't move or make a sound, no matter what. I'll come and get you when I think it's safe." Then he tacked on an afterthought. "And leave your shotgun with me. You could shoot somebody by mistake."

Swigley snorted. "Don't seem logical that Waggoner would follow this far just to do me in."

"He was willing to in town, in front of people. What makes you think he'd hesitate out here?"

It rather settled the matter in Swigley's mind, and he protested no further. They had another cold meal, and the light was fading fast, and Colley took Swigley out about seventy yards, found a depression in the earth, and told him to bed down there and not to make a damned sound. He searched the man for smoking tobacco and matches and took both away from him because he didn't want Swigley giving in to his yearnings and getting killed because of it.

"I'll come for you," Colley said again. "Don't move. I can't warn you enough on that score."

"I got some sense," Swigley said. "You won't hear a sound."

"All right," Colley said, and went back to his own camp. He made certain the horses were on well-driven picket pins, then got all the blankets and rolled them and punched them into shape so that it looked like men were rolled in for the night, one on each side of the trampled area.

Satisfied, Colley took his rifle and laid it beside one blanket roll, and Swigley's shotgun went by the other, the way a sleeping man would place his weapon, handy, yet so that he wouldn't roll on it.

Then he took care to leave the area; it was almost fully dark, and he moved around and ended up near where the horses were picketed, stretching out in the grass so that he became invisible. The horses faunched a bit, then got used to him there near their feet and quieted down, which was what he wanted.

He rested his head on his forearm, dozing in snatches, sleeping with half an ear tuned to any unusual sound. Around him the night was full of small sounds—the flutter of wings as an owl swooped down on a mouse. These were good sounds and told him that all was well, and they lulled him to sleep.

He woke often and wondered what time it was. Late—he was sure of that, because a deep chill was creeping into the air, and that meant that it was after one o'clock. And he listened and heard nothing save a deep stillness and the night breeze stirring the grass.

That was his warning, and he did not sleep after that, and for a good twenty minutes he lay there, making no sound, breathing through his open mouth, waiting for Waggoner, who was very near now.

Then he saw a deep shadow shape stir, rise like some ghost from the earth and, bent over, move soundlessly toward the blanket rolls. To move too quickly now would be a fatal mistake, Colley knew, so he waited, and when Waggoner bent down to lift the rifle from beside the blankets, Colley said, "Your mistake, Joe."

Instantly, it seemed, Waggoner wheeled and fired, and his aim was so accurate that he hit the pack horse, not four feet from where Dan Colley lay. The animal grunted and started to fall; Colley heard but did not see this, for he knew that Waggoner would shoot, and he had closed his eyes so as not to be blinded by the muzzle flash.

He rolled out of the way of the fallen horse, drew and cocked his .44. He saw Waggoner, positioned him, lined the muzzle, and closed his eyes and fired, figuring that Waggoner's vision was still not too sharp because of the muzzle flash of his own shot.

But on the heels of his own shot, Colley bounded to one side, for Waggoner's second shot cut the grass exactly where Colley had lain. I'd have stopped that one, Colley thought, and pulled his second shot slightly to one side of Waggoner's last muzzle flash.

He heard Waggoner grunt, then swear loudly, and he wondered if he'd actually hit the man or if this was one of Waggoner's tricks. It was hard to tell, and a man would be a fool to bound up and run and take a look.

Colley fell silent and listened; he could hear the labor of Joe Waggoner's breathing, but that didn't prove a damned thing; any man could pant convincingly.

He couldn't see Waggoner, for the man was down in the grass, or he was behind one of the blanket rolls; either way he was well hidden and doubly dangerous.

Finally Waggoner said, "You got lucky, Colley. Colley, did you hear what I said?"

I heard you, Colley thought, but didn't answer, for Waggoner wanted a sound to shoot at, and to a man who knew what he was doing, that was as accurate as broad daylight with a full view. There had been a time in his life when he hadn't believed such a thing possible, but men coming back from the war had taught him different. One day, on a bet, one of Texas's war-bred gunfighters had bet another a hundred dollars a shot that he could hit cowbells with his six-shooter in a pitch-dark room. A hundred dollars paid for every one hit and double that for each one missed.

That gunfighter had cleaned out half the gamblers in town before they woke up to the fact that it was a case of good ears and no trick.

"Colley?" A moment of silence. "Where's the farmer, Colley?"

On his belly now, Colley was moving slowly, silently to a new spot; then he cupped his hands around his mouth and threw his voice back, where he had been. "Safe enough, Joe."

Instantly Waggoner shot, sending his bullet in the spot Colley had vacated, and Colley answered his fire just as quickly, for he had the gunman spotted now and an instant's advantage; he shot one time and heard Waggoner grunt, and then there was a thrashing of legs on the ground and the sound of gagging, and Colley knew that this was no trick.

Still he stayed down, out of sight, and moved again, carefully, stirring no grass and making no sound. He knew that some men would have reloaded and charged Waggoner, fanning down a layer of fire, and he knew that this was a quick way to get killed.

Waggoner wasn't dead, and he was the kind that would shoot once and put his bullet into the part that counted. He knew Waggoner, knew Waggoner's kind; they were a cold, careful, methodical lot that didn't do a lot of shooting but made it count when they did.

He remembered back in Texas some years past when a tough holed up in a line shack with a repeating Henry rifle, six boxes of shells, and a grim determination to hold off anyone who tried to take him. After one man had been killed and three wounded and the tough had shot up half his shells, someone thought to ride into the next county and bring back a Texan named Longley who had a reputation for pretty accurate and quick shooting.

A lot of people fell out to see that, and Longley disappointed them. Four rounds from a Sharps brought down the smokestack, and in a few minutes the door came open, billowing smoke, followed by the tough who ran out levering and firing his Henry with reckless abandon.

Longley had then fired one shot, and that was it. He collected his fifty dollars and went back home.

So Dan Colley wasn't in any hurry to charge Waggoner and get killed. He lay there for a good twenty minutes, listening to the painful sawing of Waggoner's breathing. Now and then he would hear retching, as though Waggoner were vomiting, but Colley said nothing, made no sound at all.

"Colley? I'm—gut shot!"

Colley figured that that was the truth all right, but Waggoner could still cock and squeeze off. All he could do was wait and let Joe Waggoner make the next move. He could see the man, down behind a blanket roll, yet not completely covered by it.

After thinking about it for a moment, Colley

decided to risk a little just to see how helpless Waggoner was. He held his gun out to one side as far as he could, aimed carefully although not accurately and then squeezed off.

The bullet struck near Waggoner, and immediately Waggoner fired at the muzzle flash, the bullet cutting the grass two feet from Colley's head.

Now I know, Colley thought, and reloaded his gun.

There was more silence, and then Colley heard Waggoner turning the cylinder, reloading, too. Waggoner said, "Let's—talk. What's Swigley—to you, Colley? Better my—way."

He was trying to move, to drag himself to another position, and he grunted in pain, and then Colley bellied along in the grass, sure that Waggoner wouldn't hear him. Now and then he would stop and look, and Waggoner was still there, and Colley worked around until he was directly behind the man.

Then he started moving in, a few inches at a time, and after a while no more than ten feet separated them, and Colley knew that Waggoner, hurt the way he was, couldn't possibly whirl around in time to exchange shots.

So he said, "I'm behind you, Joe. Don't move! I'll blow a hole right through your spine!" He stood up, and three jumps later he kicked the gun out of Waggoner's hand, then bent and searched him for other weapons. There was blood on the man's side, soaking his shirt and brush jacket, and another sticky patch on his thigh.

Satisfied that Waggoner had no other gun or a knife, Colley holstered his own pistol and quickly kicked some dead brush together and made a fire. As the light spread, he could see Waggoner's eyes, glazed now with pain.

Colley said, "You know I can't do a damned thing to help you, Joe. And I'm sorry."

"Got a drink?" Waggoner asked.

"Water."

"A man—hadn't ought to—die with that on— his stomach." He smiled, and blood oozed past the corner of his mouth. "I could have—taken you in a stand—up fight."

"Too late to find out now," Colley said. "Joe, I was willing to leave you alone. What was it with you, anyway?" He squatted down and picked up a canteen and uncapped it. Then he offered it to Waggoner, thinking that the man wouldn't really refuse it, but he did. Colley drank, capped it, and put it aside. "Did you want what I had? Is that it? Men feared you, Joe. Wasn't that enough?" He got no answer and looked carefully at Waggoner; then he noticed the vacant stare in the man's eyes and knew that it was all over.

It saddened him, not because he had killed Waggoner, but because the man was dead; he no longer existed and had left nothing behind to be remembered by. His land would be cut up and gobbled up by his neighbors before the snow fell; they'd quarrel and fight over it, and next year at this time they wouldn't remember who it had belonged to.

Dan Colley stood up and yelled, "Swigley! Oh, Swigley! Come on in! It's all over now! We're going back!"

And this bothered him because he didn't think it was important at all now that Swigley would get his fair trial. A man had died, alone, without a friend, and instead of ending anything, Colley had the gnawing feeling that it was the start.

4

Because his place was on the way back, Dan Colley stopped, and it was midafternoon, and some of the crew was at the corral where the saddle string was being gentled. Everything stopped because Joe Waggoner was tied face down across his saddle, and trouble was an odor on the wind.

Colley's wife came out, a hand raised to shield her eyes from the strong sunlight, and he waved her back into the house. When Scotty came up, Colley said, "You keep Swigley here. Have some fresh horses saddled. We're on our way to town."

"Be better if the sheriff came here."

"Do as you're told," Colley said with no anger at all, and walked wearily to the house. He was dirty, and he needed a shave, but there was no time for these niceties. There was coffee in the kitchen, and he got a cup, then leaned against the sink. Edith watched him a moment, and finally he said, "I'd like to know ahead of time how Al Ritchie is going to take this."

"Do you care?"

"Well, no, I guess, but a man likes to sidestep trouble when he can."

"Not with Al."

He frowned and studied her. "You don't like him, do you?"

"I never did. I never will. He sicked Waggoner after you."

Dan Colley shrugged. "Maybe. But Waggoner wanted to go." He sighed and raked his fingers over his beard. "Of course, it was more than Swigley; it always has been. But with Al I don't know. He seemed to calm down for a while, Edith. Has he bothered any of the farmers in the past year or two? He hasn't, and you know it."

"Only because he was afraid of you," she said quickly.

He laughed. "That's nonsense!"

"Is it? Two years ago he had twenty men, and he wasn't sure how it would turn out if he openly bucked you. Now he's got forty men, and some of them are as mean as Waggoner was. He's trying you, Dan, feeling you out. This thing over Swigley could have been settled by now, only Al Ritchie wouldn't let it be. He knew it would bring you into it, and it was his way of finding out how far you'd go. If he thinks he can push you, he'll do it." She came over to him and put her arms around his waist. "Dan, I love you, and I know what you stand for and believe in. But it's too soon, Dan. Maybe in another ten years—"

He kissed her and put her away from him. "I can't wait ten years. Right now I've got to go into town with Waggoner and Swigley before Sheriff McLimas has a warrant sworn out for me for jailbreak."

"Dan, don't let Ritchie surprise you."

He looked at her and smiled. "I didn't let Joe Waggoner, did I?"

Then he went outside and mounted the fresh horse Scotty had brought up and turned to the town road. Swigley said nothing for a while, then, "I sure don't relish going back to jail, Mr. Colley."

"You're safer there."

Swigley turned and looked at Waggoner. "Hope there's no trouble over this."

"There's always trouble when a man is killed," Colley said. "Now shut up because I don't feel like talking."

This offended Swigley, hurt his feelings; he felt that after all they had been through together they should have been pals. And he believed that Colley had done everything out of some personal regard; Swigley had neither the personality nor the mind to accept any other explanation.

They arrived in town just as the last of the daylight was fading, and their arrival caused a stir. Merchants hurried out to see everything, and by the time Colley and Swigley had traveled half the length of the street, they had a following.

Al Ritchie was still in town; he came out of the trading post and stood on the porch, watching Colley dismount, then he came across the street as Sheriff Ora McLimas came out of the hotel. Ed Gruen, the deputy, was down the street some-where, and he came on the run as soon as he heard that Colley and Swigley were back.

McLimas had Waggoner lifted off the horse and placed on the sidewalk; he looked at him briefly, then said, "He's got a few holes in him, Dan."

"He could have let it go any time," Colley said. "I gave him the chance."

"Did you?" Al Ritchie asked, and Colley whipped his head around. "I was just asking the question, Dan. We all knew Waggoner. And we know you. It's kind of a question of who jumped who."

"You guess," Colley said.

"I'm waiting for you to say," Ritchie put in. "That's my man there, dead. You think I can go back to the ranch and tell the others I did nothing?"

"There's nothing you can do now," Colley said. He looked at Ike Swigley. "You forget, Al, I have a witness."

There was no way for Al Ritchie to know that Swigley had been too far away to be a witness to anything, although he had heard the shooting, but the notion hit him suddenly, and it made him back off. "Hell of a note," he said fretfully, "a man getting killed over a damned farmer!" With that he turned and went across the street to Dunfee's and went inside.

Sheriff McLimas was pulling the ends of his waterfall mustache. "I take it this was an up-and-up fight, Dan. I see he's got all the holes in front." He shrugged his meaty shoulders and motioned for two men to help him. "Let's get him down to the doc's. The rest of you people go on about your business. Gruen, lock your prisoner up again."

Gruen nodded and took Swigley by the arm as though he were pretty surprised to have him back in custody again. Gruen had a swollen place at the corner of his mouth where Colley had hit him, and he touched this as though to remind Colley that he hadn't forgotten it.

The crowd started to thin and Colley pushed through and crossed the street. Louis Bergerac was sweeping off the walk; he squinted at Colley and grinned. "You done the county a favor, Dan. I've never seen a man deader."

"You think that's good, Louis?"

Bergerac shrugged. "I'd have took his hair." He nodded toward the inside. "Ritchie didn't take it so good, did he? He ain't much of a sport when you come right down to it."

"Who the hell is?" Colley asked, and went on inside.

Dunfee was tending the bar, and he poured a shot of whiskey into a tin cup as Colley came up. Al Ritchie stood with his forearms heavy on the bar, and he spoke without turning his head.

"I want to ask you something, Dan. Which was the one we could stand to lose? Swigley or Waggoner?"

"Now I don't have much use for either of 'em," Colley admitted. He drank and made a face and set the cup down. "Jesus, Dunfee, this is terrible stuff!" Then he looked at Ritchie, who was staring. "You just don't understand, do you, Al?"

"No. Explain it to me."

"Just this once," Colley said. He turned and leaned so that he faced Ritchie. "This was Indian country until the cattlemen decided to take it. But we don't have an exclusive right to it, either, so the farmers came along. Swigley is a poor farmer, but then Waggoner was more gunman than cowboy. Show me the difference."

"He was on our side!" Ritchie snapped. "Damn it, Colley, there *are* sides!"

"Yes, or so it seems. But one side's not always right, Al. What do you want? All the valley? You can't have it."

"Who says so?"

"I do. Don't ever make the mistake of trying to take my part of it."

Al Ritchie straightened and stood stiffly. "You threatening me, Dan?"

"Telling you how it will be," Colley said mildly. "If you want to think I'm fooling, then it'll be your own mistake." He nodded toward Dunfee, tossed off the rest of the drink, and walked outside. Someone had tied his horse, and when he started to untie him, Bergerac eased out of the dark shadows along a building.

"It don't do a damned bit of good to tell a man like that anything. He's goin' to believe what he wants, anyway." Then he inclined his head across the street. "Look up, boy!" And then he melted back into the darkness.

Colley swung his head. Al Ritchie had come out and was teetering on the edge of the porch. He said, "Leaving just like that, Dan?"

"Just like that," Colley told him.

"Don't get on that horse. Waggoner was a friend of mine."

The tone of his voice was like an alarm bell, and farther down two men stopped and looked around, and a third joined them, and that was enough to start a crowd.

Colley said, "Al, what are you pretending? That you give a damn?" He laughed. "You don't. But you've got something stuck in your throat, so you'd better get it out."

"All right," Ritchie said and walked off the porch. "What you got was given to you. To me you haven't earned an acre of it."

"What's that to you?"

"What I make it," Ritchie said. "I'm not carrying a gun. It's in my bedroll."

"Just what's that supposed to mean?"

"I'll settle this without a gun," Ritchie said, and peeled off his coat, throwing it in the street. "I couldn't go home tonight and sleep knowing I hadn't done something for old Joe."

"Yeah," Colley said, his manner dry. "So you want to fight about it. I thought you were brighter than that. But maybe you think that if you lick me you'll gain a little weight. Friend, you just don't eat the right kind of meat."

"You take that gun off and I'll show you," Ritchie told him.

Colley shook his head, not caring what the crowd thought. He turned to the stirrup and put his foot in it. "Al, I'm tired and I'm going home and eat some of my wife's pie. Go find someone else."

"I didn't think you were scared," Ritchie said.

From the height of the saddle, Colley looked down. "Al, you just can't be *that* stupid." He kneed his horse in motion and would have ridden into Ritchie if the man hadn't moved. Ritchie hadn't wanted to do that, and it made him angry to be tricked by his own instincts. Without warning he made a jump for Colley's horse, meaning to pull him down off it, but the horse shied and Ritchie fell, sprawling in the street.

The men standing around laughed; it was a natural reaction, but it wasn't funny to Ritchie. He got up swearing, and then he picked up a handful of dust and flung it in the horse's face, making him rear.

But Colley was already whipping down out of the saddle, and he let the horse go on down the street, snorting and blowing and shaking his head. "All right, Al, if you just have to."

It was what Ritchie wanted, and he tore into Colley. His hurry made him clumsy, and he only knocked Colley's hat off and stung him on the forehead. Colley wanted to get his coat off so he stomped down on Ritchie's foot, and the man began to crow-hop around in the street, and everyone laughed at that, too.

Then Colley got shed of his coat and gun belt, draping them over the hitch rail, and he hunched his shoulders and waited while Ritchie limped some of the pain away.

"You dance pretty good," Colley said. "Why

49

don't you close in, and I'll show you a real two-step?"

Ritchie was angry, and his rage was bubbling, trying to get out. Dan Colley felt a little sorry for him because a man should lock himself in the smokehouse when he got that way and not try to fight with anyone. But he had seen a lot of men lose their tempers and sometimes they lost their lives, and if Ritchie wanted to blow up, then Colley was determined to help him.

Some of the men watching laughed; they thought all fights were funny as long as they didn't have to get in there and take any of it. Colley remained by the hitch rail, and he let Ritchie come in, and then he spun, planted his hands firmly and mule-kicked and timed it so that Ritchie ran into it.

The man did a complete somersault in the street and rolled several times before stopping, and when he got up, he did so painfully, for he had taken the blow flush on the chest, and his breathing was working like a steam calliope.

Colley looked at him, stood there waiting for him, and he felt a little sorry for Ritchie because this could end bad, almost had to if it was going to end at all. He had never seen a fight that hadn't ended that way, for there were no rules and no one would have been inclined to follow them if there had been. It was put your man down hard and put him down any way you could, and if it crippled him, it didn't matter too much, because no one really cared.

Painfully Ritchie hunched over, and he weaved a bit as he tried to walk toward Dan Colley. It was pride driving the man, nothing else. Ritchie was hurt, and there was no strength in him, and finally Colley had all he could stand of it. He said, "It's time for me to get home," and then he walked diagonally down the street, mounted his horse, and took one last look at Al Ritchie, who was suddenly sitting down in the street.

"You come back!" Ritchie yelled, his voice all pinched. "Damn you, come back!" Then he looked around and held out a hand. "I want a gun! God, somebody give me a gun!"

It was brag, just talk, Colley thought. Then some man in the crowd, someone who wouldn't have a complete day until someone got shot, took his .44 from the holster and tossed it near Al Ritchie.

Ritchie really didn't want a gun, but now there one lay, and he had to reach for it; there was nothing else he could do.

As his hand streaked out, Colley drew; there seemed to be plenty of time, and he fired and shot just under the pistol, bouncing it into the air. The crowd jumped back, and he shot again, jolting it farther down the street, and again, this time hitting it deliberately to break it.

Al Ritchie sat there like a man who has just

seen something he hadn't believed possible, like a man who has died and now lives again. Colley said, "Al, won't you ever listen to anyone?" Then his glance raised, trying to search out the man who had thrown the gun down, but that was one who wasn't about to show himself. "It wouldn't hurt any of you if you helped him," Colley said, then turned and rode rapidly down the street, sorry it had happened at all.

He was a mile out of town before he pulled the horse to a walk, and then he made a cigarette, dropping the reins to do so. There was no doubt in Dan Colley's mind now that Edith had been right, because Ritchie had made his stand and gotten pushed down, but he was too much of a fool to be stopped now. People would talk about this, and Ritchie's skin was too thin to take it. Every time someone looked at him, he'd think they were recalling the night he had been licked. Every word said out of his earshot would be talk against him, because he was that way and he had always been that way.

I can lick him, Dan Colley thought. I can outshoot him, too.

But with a man like Ritchie you had to ask yourself, could you outfight and outshoot the men he could hire?

5

Dan Colley was not a mile from town when Scotty loomed out of the night, rode past, then they both wheeled and met stirrup to stirrup. "Your wife needs the doc, Dan," Scotty said.

"I'll go back with you," Colley said, feeling a new sense of hurry.

They talked no more, and they rode rapidly, although Scotty's horse was tiring, and when Scotty began to drop back, Dan Colley didn't slow to stay with him. He reached the doctor's house first and was at the door before Scotty wheeled in and flung off.

There were lamps lit, and finally the doctor's housekeeper opened the door. She took one look at Colley and said, "A fine thing you did to Mr. Ritchie! He's got three broken ribs."

"That ought to keep him quiet for a while," Colley said, and pushed past her and opened the door to Spence's office. Ritchie was still there, stretched out on the table, and Spence was winding him tightly with bandages. He looked around, and Colley said, "You're needed at my place, doc. My wife—"

"When I'm through here. Be another ten minutes."

"Don't poke then," Colley told him, and went

out into the hall where Scotty waited. The housekeeper had gone to the rear of the house, and Scotty was walking up and down, slapping his hat against his chaps.

"He's with Ritchie now," Colley told him. "Be a few minutes. Why don't you go over to Dunfee's and have a drink? Rest your horse. You about done him in."

Scotty opened his mouth to say something, then closed it, nodded, and went out. Finally Dr. Spence came out, shrugging into his coat; he had his satchel in hand.

"My buggy's in back. Take me a minute to hitch up." He looked askew at Colley. "Been a busy night for both of us, huh?"

"I'm going on ahead. If that mare of yours wants to run, let her."

"I do on occasions like this," Spence said, and went to the rear of the house.

Colley went out the front way, mounted, and left town, hurrying now because there was a reason to, not because he had a mad to work off. He was more concerned than worried about Edith; she was a healthy girl with good bones, but this was her first child, and it was all unknown to him and somewhat frightening.

He supposed that a man didn't think about how much his wife meant to him until a time like this and the possibility of losing her reared up and stared him in the face. She was more than a woman to him. She was a life, a promise of good things, and the reason he could change himself and like that change, believe in it so much that whatever else he had believed before seemed unreal.

And it wasn't that she preached at him or argued him into anything; he had seen these things for himself because they were the right things and not always the easy things. But he supposed that most of the good things came hard to a man, especially when he had always had his own way and lived with no great responsibilities.

There were lamps burning when he reached the house, and the cook was in the kitchen; he had coffee hot in the pot. Colley flung his hat in one corner and went on into the bedroom. Edith was in bed, sweating, letting the pains come when they wanted to and not fighting them and wasting her strength that way. He sat on the edge of the bed, and she took his hand and held it tightly.

Her smile was a small one, then she said, "Now don't tell me you're sorry and all that nonsense. A baby's a baby."

"Doc Spence is right behind me. You think it's time?"

"I don't think, I know. You'll hear a squawl before morning. From me and the baby."

"This is a hell of a thing for a woman to go through," he said half angrily.

She laughed. "They've never figured out any

other way, Dan. Might as well make up your mind to it."

He stayed with her a good fifteen minutes, then he heard Spence's rig come in the yard, and he went out, meeting him as he came through the kitchen. "Right in there," Colley said, pointing to the bedroom.

"I've been here before," Spence said sourly. "Now clear the hell out. Husbands are no damned good at a time like this."

Most of the crew was up and standing around the back porch when Dan Colley came out. One of the hands said, "I just happen to have a bottle of whiskey, for medicinal use. If you feel sick or anything."

"Let's go into the cook shack," Colley suggested. "You get your medicine, and I'll see if cookie will come up with some pie." He looked back toward the house, then went on across the yard to the cook shack.

He went in ahead and lit the lamps, and one of the men said, "This will make cookie mad. He don't like no one in here unless he says so."

"He's going to be busy in the house," Colley said, and went into the pantry and began setting out peach pies. "We ought to have some coffee. Baldy, fetch some wood and get a fire going." Then he walked to the door and stood there, looking toward the house. The cook saw him through the kitchen window and came out. For a moment it looked as though he were going to yell across the yard and demand to know what the hell they were doing in his cook shack, but he remembered Edith Colley and kept his mouth shut.

Colley knew that he'd hear about it at the first opportunity, for Scorchy was as temperamental as a woman when it came to his kitchen, but that was the price a man paid for feeding his hands well.

It seemed that there was a price on just about everything.

When the coffee was done, he went in and had some, ate some pie, and took a pull from the whiskey bottle. Then he heard wagons approaching, and they all went outside to see who it was. One of the men fetched a lantern, and they met the first wagon by the well; two more pulled up and stopped.

Barney Fine was the first one down, and he hitched up his bib overalls and looked around and said, "Surprised to find you all up. Somethin' goin' on?"

"My wife's having a baby," Colley said, "so I'll thank you to keep your voices down. What are you doing here?"

Art Morley and his strapping sons joined Fine, and a man named Norris with a brood of half-wild boys edged up; there were nine in all, and most of them carried shotguns.

Fine did the talking. "We didn't know who to turn to, Colley. I fear for Swigley. He ain't safe in town."

"Swigley's a friend of yours? Since when? I didn't know he had any real friends." He looked from one to the other. "You figure if Swigley can be reached, then so can you."

"That's about right," Fine admitted. "We know the stand you took against Ritchie, and we heard what happened to Waggoner."

"That would happen to any man who set out to kill me," Dan Colley said. He looked from one to the other. "A long time ago I told you to keep your knives out of beef that didn't belong to you. Did you think I was fooling? The only thing is that Swigley figured I'd stand still if he stole one of mine."

"Well," Fine pointed out, "you married a farm girl and—"

"Don't you people understand anything?" Colley asked, feeling his temper grow short. "Let me set you straight on something. I tried to help Swigley because a man in the lockup was threatened by lynch law. It didn't make a damned bit of difference to me whether he was a farmer or not. I'd have done the same for Waggoner."

"You confuse a man," Fine said. "That kind of thinkin' don't make sense. You're either on a side or not."

"If there's no side, there's no trouble," Colley

pointed out. "You want me to make war for you? Is that it? The hell with it! Take care of yourself. You've got to learn sometime."

"That judge ain't here yet," Art Morley said. "And even if he lets Swigley go, how long do you think Ritchie will let him go free? Hell, there'll be a shot and Swigley will never know what hit him. That could be us."

"Not if you mind your own business." He waited for them to say something, and when they didn't, he nodded. "I see your point. Swigley is killed, and someone gets away with it, and you wonder who'll be next and for what reason. A good point, one I've wondered about myself. Sure, Ritchie is a hog. Men are hogs when they have the chance. You want to know whether or not you can count on me? Hell, you ought to know the answer to that."

"We know it," Fine said solemnly, "but it does a man good to hear it. We're goin' into town now to watch over Swigley. If he goes to jail—well, we'll let it go at that. But if the judge lets him off, we'll do the best we can to help him clear out before Ritchie gets to him. He's hirin' men, you know. And they all pack pistols real confidently."

"Good luck," Colley told them. "I think you're worrying for nothing, but it won't hurt to keep an eye on things."

They wanted to shake hands; farmers were big on this, while cattlemen didn't think much of it.

Then they got in their wagons and drove out of the yard, keeping the noise down.

And Dan Colley went back to waiting.

He became a father just a few minutes before the morning sun showed itself, and there was an anxious half hour before Spence came out and told him that it was a girl. One of the men whooped, then choked it off and settled for a silent war dance in the yard.

Colley's wife was fine, worn out, but fine, and Spence went to the cook shack for coffee and breakfast. Scorchy came from the house, waddling along on his twisted legs, all that remained of his bronco-riding days. He gave Colley a withering glance and said, "If you've made a mess, there'll be hell to pay."

Then he stomped off across the yard.

Colley looked in on his wife and found her asleep, and he did not disturb her. The doctor remained until well after nine o'clock, then he got into his rig and turned it toward town, letting the mare plod along while he dozed on the seat.

When Scotty came back, he told Colley that Ritchie had been taken home in a spring wagon and that the farmers had been deputized by Sheriff McLimas and that the judge was due in on the afternoon stage, which had been held up three days already by a flash flood farther south.

Dan Colley felt then that things would cool

down and he could get on with ranching, because the summers were short as it was and he had fallen a little behind with this Swigley affair. He put some of his men to work on fences in the high pasture, and he sent two men out with a wagon and block salt to put down at the licks and water holes.

There was hay and winter feed to get in because winter closed in fast, and any man that wasn't set up for it two months beforehand was in trouble, since fall roundup ran right up until the first snow.

A wagon and a crew started hauling supplies and stocking the line shacks, and Colley had six that he kept manned all winter. There was wood to cut and haul; every man on the place worked from dawn to dark. He sent Scotty out instead of going himself because he had to take care of his wife until she was able to be up and around.

And Dr. Spence, when he came back, said that wouldn't be for two weeks.

No one went to town, and Spence brought the only news, which was of Swigley's trial. Then a lawyer Colley had never seen before came out with the sheriff, introduced himself, and said that he had been appointed by the judge to defend Swigley, and did Colley want to sign the complaint or let it go?

Not signing it would give the attorney a good lever for freeing Swigley. It would also tell every jackleg rawhider passing through that he could butcher a WR steer and get away with it. But Colley weighed it all carefully in his mind and figured that if he signed the complaint and Swigley went to jail, it would satisfy Ritchie and Stoddard and Mitchell, but it would cut a rift between cattlemen and farmers that wouldn't be healed so quickly. Trouble with Ritchie didn't bother Colley because he already had that, and the events of the past eight days had taught him just how far he could count on Stoddard and Mitchell.

It was best, he figured, to let Swigley have the chance to clear out of the country. Maybe the man would learn a lesson; Colley doubted it, but the man deserved the chance.

"I'm too damned busy to fool with it," Colley told the lawyer, who then rode back to town in a jubilant frame of mind.

Sheriff McLimas stayed for supper and an excuse to talk to Dan Colley. He thought that a grave mistake had been made. "You've turned against your own kind, Dan."

"My kind? Don't lump me in with Ritchie and the rest. Damn it, Ora, can't you see that Swigley was just a handy excuse for Ritchie to move? A week ago I'd have argued that notion, but he made it clear to me the other night." He shook his head. "With Swigley gone—and I think the farmers will see that he clears out—Ritchie can't do anything without telling everyone plain enough that he's just a hog out after more graze."

"Maybe you're right about that," McLimas admitted. "But you've opened the door to farmer trouble. I tell you, Dan, unless they fear you, they have no respect."

"How do you feel about me?"

"What's that mean?"

"Are you afraid of me?" Colley asked.

"Hell, no, I ain't afraid."

"So then you don't respect me."

"Sure I do, Dan." He frowned. "Oh, I see what you're gettin' at. Still, it don't hold water with farmers. Take your wife's family; they turned her out when she married you. You or her heard from 'em since?" Dan shook his head. "Don't mean to put it personal like that, but these sod-busters are just always looking for some reason to cry that they're being picked on. Hell, they clomp down on a few hundred acres, raise a few crops, maybe clear a couple of hundred a year after everything's paid for, and act like they've got a lot of money to spend or somethin' worthwhile to contribute to the country. Why, you carry a pay-roll big enough to buy 'em all out. Ain't that so?"

"Sure, but it don't give me the right to push 'em, Ora. Little man, big man—they both have the same sized rights. Now it took me one hell of a long time to learn that, so don't figure you can argue me out of it easy."

"I kind of agree with you, but the country's too young. If a man can't take care of himself, then he's bound to get stepped on. Now you had your trouble with Ritchie, and I'd like to see it patched up. I was hoping you'd do it by signin' the complaint against Swigley."

"And I keep telling you that Swigley was only an excuse."

The sheriff sighed and shrugged. "Then Ritchie will try again, won't he? I never heard of him to back down."

"Did you ever hear of me doing it, either?"

McLimas shook his head. "Like a couple of bulls, I guess. Well, you've both got a lot to lose. Maybe that'll hold you back."

"Don't look at me. I'm satisfied with what I got. It's Ritchie that wants it all."

"Does it matter which does the wantin'? He'll reach and you'll fight back. It all means war, and I hate to see it come."

"Nothing stays peaceful forever, Ora. A man takes one look at peace, and he figures everyone's weak. It's a lesson that man has to learn over and over again, or so it seems." He tapped the sheriff on the chest. "I wouldn't go back to Laramie right away if I was you. You see my point?"

"Yes, I'm sorry to say I do."

6

Ike Swigley's trial was a disappointment to Al Ritchie, and the other ranchers, Stoddard and Mitchell, made out like it offended them, too, because they didn't want to give Ritchie the notion that they disagreed. The fact that Dan Colley didn't sign a formal complaint probably saved Swigley from hanging, but he *had* stolen and butchered a calf, and the judge gave him a year in the Laramie jail for it.

The farmers were jubilant, for in their minds this marked the beginning of a new era and the end of another where every thief was automatically hanged. But they weren't fool enough to think that it was all over, and they remained in town, guarding the express office until Sheriff Ora McLimas made ready to take the prisoner south.

Ritchie and his cattlemen friends lined the bar at Dunfee's place and loudly registered their disgust at the whole thing. Finally Sam Mitchell, who really didn't want any part of this, announced that it was late and that he had to be heading home. Doe Stoddard was of a mind to go along with him, but he was a man easily persuaded, and Ritchie kept pulling at his arm, and Stoddard stayed.

"The law in this county," Ritchie announced,

"has plumb gone to hell." He looked around, for most of the men there rode for him, and the rest were Stoddard's, and he didn't expect any disagreement. "You mark my words now—we're going to have farmer trouble. They'll start getting bold, and when the day comes when a farmer figures he can walk on the same sidewalk with you, then you've got trouble."

They agreed with this, for they had a mounted man's sense of superiority, and the causes for this ran generations back, so far that they did not understand the beginning of it all. The Roman leaders rode so that they towered over their legions, and slave masters rode so that their whip could more easily fall on the backs of the workers. Authority was elevated; even on a ship the captain trod his quarterdeck and stood higher than the crew in the well deck. A man who had anything to say always stood up while the listener remained seated, and just about everyone had been "on a soapbox" a few times in his life.

"McLimas will take Swigley back on the stage," Ritchie said. "And that won't be for another three or four days. That gives us some time, anyway."

"To do what?" Doe Stoddard asked.

"Never you mind," Ritchie said. "Let's get out of here." He turned to the door and went out, his men following him, and they mounted up with a loud run of talk and stormed out of town.

Stoddard and four of his men remained in the place, and he sighed and finished his drink, then laid his money on the bar. Dunfee had been at the far end of the room; he heard the coin and came around to his side of the bar.

Dunfee said, "Bet you got a lot of work at your place this time of year, huh, Doe?"

"A man just never seems to get caught up," Stoddard agreed.

"Then I'd try," Dunfee advised. "I'd get so busy I wouldn't have time for Al Ritchie."

"Oh, hell, he's all right. A little headstrong, but I can handle him." He laughed and waved his hand and walked out, and his men followed him; they mounted up and rode out of town immediately.

Stoddard's place was seven miles to the west, an impressive piece of rangeland, and most everyone held to the opinion that if Stoddard tended a little more to business he'd someday be a wealthy man. But it just wasn't in him to work much harder than it took to get by. His place was big enough for him to have to keep fifteen men on the payroll all winter and double that in the summer, but he had the reputation of running an easy ranch, and the riders who wanted to take life easy always hired on with Doe Stoddard because he never worked anyone very hard.

When he reached his place, he had one of the men take his horse to the barn, and then he went inside the house, a low, log affair that had been added onto and then added on some more until the character of it was confused. It was built in the shape of a U because that was easier than taking out three large trees.

Stoddard's wife was no longer a young woman, yet life had not reduced her to a wreck, simply because long ago she had decided not to kill herself making up for what he did not do. His two sons were almost grown, and the girl was going on fifteen and beginning to fill out to woman-size.

"Expected you back earlier," his wife said when he came in and washed at the sink. "They goin' to hang him?"

He shook his head and dried his face. "A year in jail. Too easy for him, I say."

"Nobody listens to what you say, Doe."

He didn't like to have her talk like that in front of his children, but she had been doing it a long time, and he didn't know what to do about it. "Ain't you boys got chores? Go on now. Don't want you loafin' around the house. Ma'll call you for supper."

"No danger of 'em missin' a meal," she said, and watched them go out. "Dan Colley come in for the trial?"

Stoddard shook his head. "Damned man any-way, backing out that way! I don't understand, it. He's got as much to lose as any of us. Ritchie is right, you know. The farmers will start thinkin' equal now. You wait and see." He looked at his daughter. "One of those farm boys ever make an eye at you when you're in town, you just let me know, you hear?"

"Now don't go startin' to worry about that," his wife said. "I want you to stay plumb out of anything that Ritchie means to do, Doe. You hear what I say now? Don't go ridin' off with that man. He'll get you into something that you can't get out of."

"I can handle myself," Stoddard maintained. "Damn it, how many times I got to tell you that?" Her attitude offended him, and he stomped out and stood on the back porch awhile, then walked toward the corral to look at the horses.

It was a damned shame, he thought, when a man had to live with a woman who was always questioning his judgment. Hell, he hadn't done so bad for her. He'd come up from Texas with a trail herd as a young man, one of the first to go north after the war, and he'd seen country he'd never known existed, and it kind of took him, this traveling fever.

He'd tried some mining in the Arizona country, and horse hunting in Utah, and he'd even gone to Nevada for a spell. He couldn't recall what had taken him into Wyoming, but the land was there, and he'd settled down on it and decided to get a wife.

It was quite natural for him to go to Texas for her; he wanted a woman who was his kind, but he had little to offer—just the land and the cabin and a herd of cattle. So he'd taken a widow with three small children, and there hadn't been time for love; she'd found him a straightforward man and believed that he would be good to her and not beat the children, and he'd found her a good woman who would care for him and not regret being his wife.

Stoddard was not sorry he had married her. He was often annoyed at her, but that was all. Because he never put much real effort into anything, he found that he loved her, and he supposed she loved him. And the children were as his own, and he could not recall thinking of them as another man's. They called him Pa because they wanted to; it just wasn't in him to insist upon anything.

When she called him for supper, he'd gotten over his pique, and afterward he went to the bunkhouse to give the hands their orders for tomorrow. He never liked to do that, but they were falling behind, and it was prod them a little now or be in trouble when winter came.

He stayed a bit and talked with them, then started back toward the house just as a rider came into his yard. They met near the barn, and Stoddard said, "What are you doing here, Dollarhide?"

"Got a message from Ritchie. He wants to meet you at the meadow spring on his place before dawn."

"What for?"

Dollarhide laughed. He was a rangy man who carried a pistol on his hip and another in a shoulder holster under his left arm, and he had a reputation with both. He was a Texas man, one of Ritchie's recent imports, and no one in the valley tried to fool themselves into thinking that Dollarhide made his living working cattle.

"He'll tell you when you get there, Stoddard."

"Hell, I just can't up and—"

"You be there," Dollarhide cut in.

This made Stoddard angry, and he let it show. "See here, you can't come on my place and order me around. Now damn it—"

Dollarhide kneed his horse close, bent in the saddle, and fisted a handful of Doe Stoddard's shirt. "Now listen here, you sonofabitch, it's no matter to me about you. I've killed four or five like you, and you know what I charged? Twenty-five dollars apiece. That's how easy it was, and that's all they were worth to me. I'd kill you for ten." He released Stoddard's shirt. "Now you be there like Ritchie says."

With that he backed his horse, turned, and rode out, and Stoddard watched him go, feeling fear wash over him like a raw wind. He knew that he ought to defy Ritchie, tell the man to go to hell, but he knew that he wouldn't. It would mean trouble, and he couldn't handle that because he'd never been a violent man. Sure, he'd talked big and all that, but he'd just never settled his troubles with violence.

The problem that bothered Stoddard the most was how he was going to get away from the place without getting his wife in an uproar; he mulled over ten or fifteen excuses and found them all bad. It was a three-hour ride to the meadow spring on Ritchie's place, and to get there before dawn he'd have to leave by two o'clock.

While he thought about it, streaks of heat lightning split the sky, and thunder rolled in booming waves, shattering and echoing, and then it started to rain. He went into the house then; his wife was in the parlor, sewing. Stoddard said, "Damned rain anyway! I'm going up into the Deer Creek section. That cabin roof leaks, and things are liable to get ruined."

She looked at him curiously. "Can't you send someone el—"

"Want it done right, then do it yourself," he said, and disappeared into the bedroom. He got his slicker and blanket roll and would have taken his rifle, too, only this would make her ask what he was doing with it, and he wasn't sure he wouldn't fumble the answer. So he left it, kissed her briefly and then splashed across the yard to the barn and his horse.

There was no fence separating his land from Al Ritchie's; Stoddard wished that there were because Ritchie's steers were always eating off some of Stoddard's best graze, but every time fence was mentioned, Ritchie took it as a personal affront. That was one thing about Dan Colley; you could talk to him and find him pretty reasonable. The idea of the fence had made sense, and Colley had split the cost of material and labor with Stoddard where the two lands joined; then he had gone on on his own and fenced Ritchie off.

Well, Colley could face up to Ritchie and get away with it; he had the nerve and the skill to do a thing like that. Ritchie hadn't liked the fence, and a couple of times he swore that he'd knock it down, but he never did.

Stoddard wished that there were time to ride over to Colley's place and tell him that Ritchie was up to something, but there wasn't, and Stoddard put it out of his mind. Maybe he should have sent one of the men over, but that thought was too late now, for he was already three miles away from his house, and he couldn't turn back.

The meadow spring was in the high country, at the head of a short, steep pass, not far from one of Colley's corner markers. There a line cabin there, for Ritchie summered part of his herd there, and as Stoddard approached the place, he could see no lights at all. But as he got into the yard, he noticed lamplight peeking through several holes in the blankets that had been hung over the windows.

The door opened and Dollarhide came out, pistol in hand. Stoddard put up his horse in the lean-to, then walked to the cabin and went in, squinting because the light hurt his eyes. He hung up his poncho and went to the fire to dry out a little.

Al Ritchie sat at the table, playing cards with Roan Teal, another Texan who had hired on at the same time Dollarhide had. Ritchie said, "I knew you wouldn't disappoint me, Doe."

"I didn't like the way Dollarhide asked."

Ritchie made a face. "He's sometimes blunt, but he gets his point across."

Dollarhide came in. "He's alone," the gunman said, and poured some coffee for himself.

Stoddard looked at Ritchie, hurt and surprised. "What the hell did you think, anyway?"

"I never chance anything if I can help it, Doe. You can't blame me for being cautious." His pleasant manner faded. "Don't get sore with me, Doe. I don't like it."

"Hell, ain't I got any rights?"

"You?" Ritchie laughed. "What the hell are you talking about?" He looked at Stoddard's bedroll, then said, "Where's your gun?"

"I didn't bring one. Should I have?"

Roan Teal looked up. "Kind of stupid, ain't he, Al?"

"I never claimed he was bright. But he'll do. Get Doe some coffee, Dollarhide."

"Let him get it himself."

Trouble hung like an old coat that no one claimed, and Stoddard got up and went to the sheet iron stove and poured his own coffee. Then he said, "What are you going to do, Al?"

"Take Swigley and the sheriff off the stage."

It was a stunning thing to hear; Stoddard stared a moment. "Why, you can't do that! McLimas will fight. He's old, but he's no coward."

"He'll be no trouble," Roan Teal said. "I get fifty dollars for shooting old sheriffs, and I'll give him an even draw." He looked at Stoddard and grinned. "You sick or somethin'?"

"Sick? God, yes, I'm sick. Al, if you think I'll have a part in this, you've got another think coming!"

"Oh, you'll go along," Ritchie said. "What the hell, you were for taking him out of jail and hanging him awhile back."

"I wasn't for it! I went along, that's all!"

"And you'll go along this time," Ritchie said evenly.

"But you don't *need* me!"

"Quit yellin'," Ritchie warned. "That's right, Doe, I don't need you. But if you're there, a part of it, you'll keep your mouth shut. You've heard me talk. I wouldn't want you pointin' a finger."

"My God, man, they'll catch up with us!"

"Who?" Dollarhide asked. "The sheriff'll be dead, and that deputy, Ed Gruen, is nothing. He can't find his butt with both hands." He laughed softly. "And your old lady will cover for you, won't she, Stoddard? She'd do that for you, wouldn't she?"

Al Ritchie considered the whole thing settled. "We'll ride southeast after daybreak. The stage is leaving around ten, so we'll catch it in the badlands. I know just the place. It'll work out all right. No one is going to see us."

Stoddard put his coffee down; he couldn't drink it now. "Al, for God's sake—"

"Aw, shut up," Ritchie said. "You whine all the damned time."

"Al, you can't want Swigley that bad," Stoddard said.

"Swigley? Who the hell is he? I want Dan Colley, friend, and if I get Swigley and the sheriff, it'll make Colley mad enough to do something. He won't know for sure, but he'll suspect, and that's enough for me." He looked at Doe Stoddard. "I want his place. Yours, too, but I'll just have to tell *you* to get out, won't I?" He laughed at the joke and flung open the door and stood there, watching the rain come down, waiting for the first dawn light to break.

7

The rain slacked off in the early morning, but Doe Stoddard didn't care. His misery was not caused by the weather. They were all hidden in the rocks that sided the road as it slashed through a section of the badlands. Teal and Dollarhide were across the road, and Stoddard and Ritchie crouched down on the east side. Ritchie had his rifle under his poncho, and when the rain stopped, he brought it out and held it across his knees.

Finally he heard what he had been listening for—the rattle of the stage as it dragged up the incline. When it pulled into view, Ritchie raised his rifle, and so did Dollarhide; they fired almost together, and the lead horses fell in their tracks, and the rest of the team stumbled, and the stage came to a halt amid a jumble of harness.

The driver threw his hands up, and Teal yelled, "No guns, sheriff! We'll riddle the coach, and some innocent people will get hurt!"

A woman whimpered in terror, and a man inside the coach soothed her. Ritchie had not exposed himself, and Dollarhide and Teal were hidden; only the muzzles of their rifles were visible to the stage driver.

Cupping his hands around his mouth, Ritchie

yelled, "Sheriff, you and the prisoner step down! Driver, cut away those horses and get going. You can make it with four. A little slower, but then you're in no hurry."

McLimas got down with Swigley handcuffed to him; they stood by the side of the road while the driver and male passengers worked to clear the harness and move enough rocks so that the stage could get through. Then the driver and passengers remounted and drove on, and Ritchie let them get on down the road a good piece before moving.

He prodded Stoddard with the rifle. "All right, let's go down. Damn it, move!" Dollarhide and Teal climbed down to the level of the road, and Ritchie and Stoddard joined them there.

McLimas looked from one to the other. "So! I thought it was you, Al, but I'm surprised to see *you* here, Doe." Swigley tried to stand behind the sheriff, like a small boy afraid of strangers. This offended McLimas, and he jerked him around to the side. "Stand like a man, damn it! There's nothin' you can do."

"Let's have the keys to the handcuffs," Ritchie said.

"I mailed them on ahead."

"Bullshit," Ritchie said. "You were on the mail stage. I won't ask you again."

"They're on the stage," McLimas said. "What the hell, do you think this is the first prisoner I ever transported? I know how it's going to be, so what difference does it make?" His gun was in his hip holster, and he went for it with a suddenness that did not fit his age; he was a fast old man without a trace of fear in him, and he almost made it, except that Teal and Dollarhide were professionals. They seemed to fire at the same time, and the old man was plucked off his feet; he fell and nearly pulled Swigley down with him. The sheriff's gun went off, but the bullet whined harmlessly in the rocks. He died there, quickly and in no pain and without one small compromise to the things he had always believed.

Dollarhide looked at him, then said, "You can't hang the little shit when he's handcuffed to the sheriff."

"Oh, it don't make that much difference," Al Ritchie said, and fired his rifle from the hip. The heavy Spencer bullet mauled Swigley flat, and he did not twitch or stir. "Get the horses, Teal. We'll pay a call at his place. They've been in this country too damned long as it is."

Doc Stoddard started to throw up, and he stood there, bent over, heaving himself dry. Mitch Dollarhide said, "Jesus, there's nothin' to him at all, is there?"

Then he went with Teal to get the horses.

Ritchie moved a few paces away, and then Stoddard wiped his face with a handkerchief and started to turn. "Where the hell you going?"

"I don't know," Stoddard said. "I don't care."

"Doe, you just can't make up your mind, can you? Right now you want to tell Dan Colley everything, but you know I'd kill you if you did that. You're not worth a good damn, but still you just can't throw yourself away, can you?" He laughed. "Don't worry about it. After we run the Swigley brood out, you can go home. All right?"

"Nothin' will ever be all right again," Stoddard said.

They came with the horses and mounted up; there was no suggestion that they bury either man, and Stoddard was too numb to make it, and a little afraid too.

"That stage wasn't so far away that they didn't hear the shots," Roan Teal said. "They'll likely come back."

"We'll be gone," Ritchie said, and led out.

It was nightfall before they drew in sight of Ike Swigley's poor parcel of land; they stopped some distance from the cabin, and Ritchie slipped a bandanna over the lower half of his face; Dollarhide and Roan Teal did the same.

Then Ritchie said, "Hitch up the team to the wagon and be quiet about it. Move it into the yard then fire the barn. When I see it go, I'll run 'em all out of the house and fire that. You come with me, Stoddard. Better put your bandanna over your face, unless you don't care who sees you."

Dollarhide and Teal moved off on a tangent, and Ritchie and Stoddard waited. Finally they saw the team and wagon being led out, then Ritchie moved on in, making sure that Doe Stoddard sided him all the way.

They made no noise as they moved into the yard; then there was a rush of flame from the hay-mow, and Ritchie fired a bullet through the window, aiming high. "Come on out of there! Your barn's afire!"

Children started crying, and a woman yelled at them. Then the door opened, and they rushed out, the woman still in her nightgown and the children frightened and half asleep. She saw the barn going up and covered her mouth to keep from crying out.

Ritchie said, "There's your wagon hitched and ready. Git and keep going!" He got down and gave the woman a push and one of the boys a kick, then went into the house and smashed a lamp and in a moment had the room ablaze.

The woman was herding the children toward the wagon, and Teal politely held the team while they all got in. Then he gave the near horse a smart lick with his quirt and set them to running.

The barn was a pyre of flying sparks, and the house was going up like old boxwood. They gathered by the well curbing, and then Ritchie said, "Go on home, Doe. Your wife's probably wonderin' what the hell's happened to you."

Stoddard looked at Al Ritchie and said, "I never knew you before today."

"Just get out of here. I don't have to tell you to keep your mouth shut."

For a moment Stoddard hesitated; he was like a man who has come upon a terrible accident, unsure whether he should run for assistance or remain and try to help.

Then he turned his horse and rode away, walking the horse, as though time no longer meant anything to him. Mitch Dollarhide let him get to the edge of the yard, then said, "I ought to shoot him now, Al."

"Now, naw, you wouldn't get anything out of it. He's too scared to do anything." He thumped Dollarhide on the arm. "Now McLimas, he had guts; he was willing to go if he could take one along. Stoddard couldn't do that if he could take all of us. The more worthless you are, the harder it is to make the trade. Come on, let's get back to the place."

Dan Colley was having his noon meal in the kitchen; Edith had fixed it, the first since the baby, for she was up and about and feeling like her old self, and she wanted to show him that she was strong again and didn't have to be waited on hand and foot. Scorchy, who had been running his cook shack and managing the house kitchen, too, made a big hooraw over the fact that he no longer would be worked to death, but he fooled no one, for he had enjoyed his role as male nurse and spent a lot of time making broth and soup and carrying trays to Edith Colley.

Scotty came into the kitchen, his manner grave. "Barney Fine's headin' this way in his wagon. He seems in a hurry."

"Tell him to come in as soon as he ties up," Colley said, and put some more pepper on his fried potatoes.

A few minutes later Fine came across the porch. He took off his hat, bowed, and gave Edith a little smile. "Good to see you up again. The first is the hardest. Could I talk to you, Dan?"

"Sure, sit down. Coffee? Edith, get Barney a plate, too." He looked at the farmer. "Some trouble? Seems like you never come here unless there's trouble."

"Yes, I guess that's Gospel," Fine admitted. "Four men ran Swigley's family off last night. Burned them to the ground."

"Was anyone hurt?"

Fine shook his head. "No, they hitched up the wagon and let them take that. But that's all. No clothes, no nothing."

Edith set a plate before him, and he nodded his thanks. She looked at her husband but said nothing; he was sitting there, his brow furrowed. "I know better than to ask whether or not they know who did it."

"Handkerchiefs over their faces," Barney Fine said. "Four of them, though."

"What about the horses? A man can disguise himself, but a horse is just as identifiable as a man."

Fine shook his head. "Hell, a horse is a horse to a farmer. If one is husky enough to pull a plow, then we look at him. If he ain't, we pay him no mind. Besides, what do you expect a frightened woman to see? Dark, and she's scared."

"You're right," Colley said gravely. "Well, it means one thing to me: Ike Swigley is dead. No one would have moved if he hadn't been."

Fine had been eating; he stopped and color left his face. "Dan, I know you wouldn't say a thing like that unless you felt sure, but could you be mistaken?"

"I could be, but I don't think I am. Where's Swigley's family now?"

"Over to Art Morley's place. It's a bit crowded because he's got a brood of his own and—" He stopped talking, for Colley had gotten up from the table and was stepping out the back door, calling for his foreman.

Then he stepped back inside, and a moment later Scotty came in. Quickly Colley told him what had happened. "Now what I want to know is whether or not we've got six men we can spare for a little milk-of-human-kindness work?"

"Sure," Scotty said. "Jingles and his crew are about through with bog riding; I expect they'll be back late today."

"First thing in the morning, then, have a wagon and building tools loaded and get over to the Swigley place. There's some timber in his north forty. Have Jingles and his crew build a new house and barn. We've got nails and hardware and some window frames in the tack shed." He looked at Barney Fine. "You go back and get all the help you can. Ask your friends if they can spare pieces of furniture, pots, pans, dishes, anything to get the Swigleys back to house-keeping."

Barney Fine thought this was mighty decent and tried to say so, but Colley waved this aside. "My reasons are a little more complex than that, Barney. I'm going to take my gun and ride over to Al Ritchie's place and tell him what we're going to do. And I'm going to tell him that if this one is burned out, I'll ride on him." He left the table and went into the bedroom for his slicker and gun belt. "Barney, I've been wrong, and I want you to know it. All along I thought peace was the absence of war. It's not. It's more than that."

Scotty said, "Got any proof Ritchie did the burning?"

Colley looked at him. "If you were going to suspect somebody, who would it be?"

"Al Ritchie. He's got a wild streak in him. No law's worth a damn unless he thought of it."

"So I'll take this to Ritchie," Colley said, and kissed his wife. "I'll be back for supper, and don't tell me to be careful. You were right. I just haven't been taking Al seriously enough. But I suppose that's because I believed that we were all right because we weren't actually shooting at each other." He clapped his hat on and shook his head. "I've been a damned fool. A stand earlier against Ritchie could have saved this. And I should have gone on to Laramie with Ike Swigley. But I didn't want to get involved further. That's one hell of an excuse for a man to have, ain't it?" He offered Barney Fine his hand. "You get your people together, Barney. I'm counting on you."

Then he went outside and Scotty ran to the barn to have a horse saddled, and when he came with it, Dan Colley swung up and cut out toward the road and Al Ritchie's place.

He was in no hurry, yet he didn't dawdle; he maintained a deliberate pace until he came to the road that turned off to Ritchie's. Then he lifted the horse into a trot and could see Ritchie's house in the distance—a cabin squatting beneath a heavy stand of timber halfway across the end of the valley.

When Colley rode into the yard, Ritchie's wife came out, a slender woman in her late twenties. Several men near the corral stopped work, and two of them walked over, and one hitched his gun belt around so that it rode a bit farther forward on his thigh.

"Edna, is Al home?"

"Asleep," she said. "He played poker all last night. I still don't know if he won anything or not."

"Wake him, will you?"

She frowned. "He won't like that, Dan."

"He's not going to like it, no matter what," Colley said.

The two men had sided his horse, and one said, "Never mind, we'll handle this. Colley— you are Colley, aren't you?—get out of here. And I won't tell you that again."

Colley looked at him, a smile glued to his face, then he freed a foot from the stirrup and kicked him in the temple. Dollarhide went down like a dropped piece of rope, and Roan Teal went for his gun, but Colley had already drawn and mashed the barrel down across Teal's head before it cleared the holster, and the man fell aspraddle of Dollarhide and remained perfectly still.

Edna Ritchie gasped; it had happened too fast for her to grasp. Colley holstered his gun and said, "You'd better wake Al now, Edna."

She kept watching and backed to the door, opened it, and without turning her head, yelled, "Al! Al, you'd better come out here! You hear me, Al?"

He heard her, and he came charging out, pulling on his pants with one hand, the other holding his gun. Then he saw Dollarhide and Teal, and he whipped his glance to Dan Colley.

"What happened?"

"They made an error in judgment," Colley said easily. "Al, I've sent a crew over to rebuild the Swigley place and move the family back in. If they have another fire or *any* kind of trouble, I'm going to come straight here to you. Understand?"

"You can't threaten me!"

"I'm telling you," Colley said. "And only once."

Then he backed his horse and rode out, using the same pace that had brought him there.

8

The bodies were brought back to town by two teamsters who found them in the road. They had met the stage farther down and learned of the holdup; still it was a shock to find the sheriff and his prisoner dead.

Ed Gruen, who liked to go to bed early, was rousted out of bed, and Doc Spence made his examination, which turned up little that everyone didn't already know, although he did find it remarkable that McLimas had been shot twice, once with a .45 and again with a .44-40.

But he drew no conclusion other than that either shot would have killed him.

Judge Scranton, who had remained over because

of an attack of "summer complaint," took the whole affair very grimly and swore that someone would be brought to justice for this because you didn't kill an officer of the law and get away with it.

But everyone figured that was just talk, and a judge had to say something like that or get people to wondering. Dan Colley heard about it because one of his men went into town with a wagon for supplies. A few days later the judge came out to Colley's place, but Dan was over to Swigley's because they were putting the roof on and Swigley's wife was about ready to move in.

A new house meant a celebration, and the word had gone out; all were invited, friend and foe alike, although Colley didn't figure that Al Ritchie or any of his crew would show up.

Judge Scranton was a gray-mannered man in his early sixties; he shook hands with Colley and got right to the point. "I don't suppose you can shed any light on this deplorable affair, Mr. Colley."

"I think I could point to the men who did it and not miss far," Colley said, "but it wouldn't be evidence." He took out his sack tobacco and offered it to the judge, who shook his head, preferring a cigar. "I've already spoken to the gentlemen, given them a warning. Like as not they'll ignore it; their intention was plain when they killed Swigley and the sheriff."

"It's not plain to me," Judge Scranton said.

Dan Colley waved his arm in a sweep that covered twenty-eight points of the compass. "That's my land. By far it's the best land within a hundred miles. We've opened up the springs, put in a few dams, and fenced a good piece of it. This land was given to me. I didn't earn it. Fact is, I didn't work it at all until a few years ago. Some men resent that. They feel that when my father died, the land should have been opened to the taker who was the strongest. Nothing is going to change their minds."

"Is any of it open range?"

Colley shook his head. "All of it owned by deed of trust or leased from the government, and there's a good eighty years to run on a ninety-nine year agreement."

"Then there's no legal grounds—"

"Judge, you know that some men feel that a six-shooter is all the legal grounds you need. And it's true, you know. Suppose someone run me off. Who'd take it back? My wife?" He shook his head again.

"Mr. Colley, I won't mince words; I've come to offer you a job."

"I figured that," Colley said, smiling, "and the answer is no."

"There's no one else. Would you say that Deputy Gruen can handle it?"

"No."

"Then who? I'd have offered it to your father."

"He'd have taken it," Colley said.

"Mr. Colley, I understand that you've just become a father. What kind of country do you want her to grow up in?"

"Judge, that's a damned unfair question."

"Certainly. What's fair about any of this? A poor farmer who steals and then is killed. A good sheriff killed. What's good about it?" He looked around at the people who were putting the finishing touches to the cabin. "Is your wife here, Mr. Colley?"

"She's over there with Mrs. Swigley. Judge, you're not going to get her going against me, are you?"

"I'm going to use every weapon I have," Scranton said. "Can you really blame me?"

"No," Colley said, and waved for Edith to come over. He introduced the judge, then said, "He wants me to be sheriff." He expected her to object immediately but she didn't.

"I suppose you've considered this carefully," she said.

"Yes, I have," Scranton said. "There's no one else, Mrs. Colley. No one at all."

"Wait a minute," Colley said, taking the judge by the arm. "I've got a man for you. Will you hear me out on this?" Scranton nodded. "Louis Bergerac. He's a kind of partner with Dunfee. You know, who has the saloon and store?"

Scranton frowned. "Are you referring to that uncouth person who wears those filthy buckskin pants and—"

"Now you said you'd hear me out," Colley reminded him. "Bergerac was a mountain man; he knows this country like the back of his hand. And I'll tell you one thing, judge, I can't think of a more dangerous man to tangle with. And I'll prove it to you."

He whistled and drew Scotty's attention; Scotty trotted over, and Colley introduced him. "I want to ask you one question, Scotty, and think carefully before you answer it. Who would be the last man in this neck of the woods that you'd like to lock horns with?"

The young man pawed his foot through the grass and scratched his head a couple of times. "Well, Dollarhide and Teal are well-known gunfighters, but I guess I'd say Bergerac. That damned old Indian could crawl up through an acre of dry leaves and never be heard, and he ain't scared of anything, man or beast. Yeah, I'd say Bergerac."

"Thanks, Scotty." Colley waited until he walked away, then looked at Judge Scranton. "Bergerac helped me break Swigley out of jail. I'd take him in preference to anyone else I know."

"But I wanted a younger man, a bright man," Scranton maintained.

"Let me put it this way: Bergerac's been smart

enough to keep his hair when this was the most dangerous Indian country in America. And he'd take the job seriously."

Judge Scranton pulled at his beard, then nodded. "All right, Mr. Colley, I'll accept your recommendation. Will you meet me in town tomorrow afternoon? We'll swear in this man as sheriff."

"I'll be there, judge." They shook hands, and Edith went back to the cabin while Colley walked over to the judge's buggy. "I'm sure you're going to be pleased with Bergerac, judge."

"I'll be pleased when these killers are hanging from a scaffold," Scranton said, and turned the rig back toward town.

"Me?" Bergerac said, leaving his mouth hang open. "Me? Sheriff?" They were in Dunfee's back room, the judge, Dan Colley, and Bergerac. "Who the hell gave you that notion?" He looked at Colley. "You did! You've been trying to get me to do respectable work for as long as I've known you. Damned meddler!"

"Now don't tell me that," Colley cut in. "You're flattered, and you know it."

Bergerac grinned and rolled his shoulders. "Well, I am at that. I'll take it if I don't have to ride with Ed Gruen."

"You can work any way you want," Judge Scranton said. "But you have some killers on the loose. They have to be caught and brought to trial. I don't want you to sentence them and execute them. Understand?"

"Yep, but you've got to give me a course in the law, judge. I know right and wrong, but sometimes laws goes against common sense."

Scranton smiled. "I think we can bring you pretty well up to date before I leave. And I can give you some books that—"

"Never mind the books. You just tell me and I'll remember. I learn best that way."

Scranton suspected that Bergerac could not read well, and he was half right, for Bergerac remembered French from his childhood and he had never learned to read or write English. Time and exposure had taught him to make out the words he needed, but he could not read a book.

"I think a public swearing-in would be in order," Scranton said. "What do you say to one o'clock in front of the store? That will give Mr. Bergerac a chance to—ah—well, bathe and change his clothes."

"I wouldn't ask for too much," Colley warned gently.

"Very well," Scranton said. "At one o'clock then."

After he went out, Bergerac gave Colley a tremendous wallop on the shoulder and grinned. "Damn you, saddlin' me with a lawman's job. It's kind of a disgrace."

"Well, you always wanted an excuse to tame some of those bucks that hang around Ritchie's spread. Here's your chance. Or was that brag?"

"You ever know me to say anything I couldn't back up?" He winked. "You wait there, sonny. I took beaver before you were born. I'll do it again."

The news that the judge was going to swear in a new sheriff got around in fast order, and Ed Gruen, when he heard it, knew that his day had arrived and got a haircut, took a bath, and appeared in his good suit.

Roan Teal came into town with some of Ritchie's riders, and they thought the whole thing was hilarious—the old Frenchman being made sheriff. They had four or five drinks to celebrate so that at one o'clock they were all staggering a little.

Ed Gruen found out the hard way that he wasn't going to be sheriff, and from that moment he became Louis Bergerac's enemy, which didn't bother Bergerac a bit, because he wanted Gruen to quit, anyway. Gruen promptly did and went inside to get drunk.

Judge Scranton administered the oath of office, and Bergerac was properly solemn through the whole affair, but Teal and his friends laughed and hooted and made a loud commotion from the porch. Then it came time to pin the badge on

Bergerac's shirt front. He said, "Excuse me, judge," and stepped toward Roan Teal. "You've got a big mouth, friend."

"Got a big gun, too," Teal said, straightening from the post he had been leaning against.

Bergerac carried no gun, and as far as Colley knew, he had never carried one. But he carried his knife; he was never without it; he wore it slantwise in a sheath right in the middle of his back belt.

Stopping ten paces from Teal, Bergerac said, "Was I you, kid, I'd go tell the judge I was sorry I was such a loudmouth. I'd 'fess up that I couldn't hold booze."

"Aw, go to hell," Teal said, and grinned. "Get away from me before I pink you. How'd you like to get an ear shot off?"

Scranton opened his mouth to assert his authority, but closed it when Dan Colley touched him on the arm.

"Now you listen to me, sonny," Bergerac said. "I can get a knife in you before you can get that six-shooter clear. So if you want it that way—"

"You've just lost that ear," Teal said and dropped his hand.

He was as good as Colley had ever seen, and he got off his shot, but not before he screamed and fell back against the wall with Bergerac's knife in his shoulder. Teal stared at it wide-eyed and grabbed the hilt, but he didn't have the nerve to pull it out.

Bergerac slipped his hand down inside his collar at the base of the neck and drew another knife, flipping it over to grip it by the blade. With one motion he included all of Teal's friends. He said, "Now you can see that I was just toyin' with the boy; I could have sunk it in his gizzard if I'd been riled. Any of you fellas think you can beat this? A few have tried." He walked up to Teal, who sagged against the wall, and before anyone could stop him, Bergerac clamped a forearm down across the gunman's chest and jerked the knife free.

Roan Teal fainted, and this seemed to disgust Bergerac. "All right, get him over to the doc's place before he bleeds all over the walk." He wiped the knife blade on his pants, sheathed both of them, and went back to where the judge stood slack-jawed.

Dan Colley said, "You still think he can't handle the office, your honor?"

"I—was honestly mistaken," Scranton said. "That young man was a gunman if I ever saw one. Didn't he have a bandage around his head, under his hat?"

"That's where I hit him with my gun barrel the other day," Colley said.

Scranton took out a handkerchief and wiped his brow. "His luck's been bad, lately, hasn't it?"

"Likely it'll turn worse," Bergerac said, coming up. He had Teal's gun, a pearl-handled forty-four-forty. "Don't see many of these. Too new. Only the professionals making big money buy the latest thing. I don't suppose there's more than three or four of these in the county. You've got a forty-four, ain't you, Dan?"

"Forty-four Smith & Wesson American," Colley said. "I expect you'll be finding out who owns the others, though."

"McLimas was shot with one of these," Bergerac said. "Not by the same man, either."

"How do you know?" Scranton asked.

"Looked at the body when it was brought into town. The forty-four-forty went in the left breast, went clean through and came out under the right shoulder. The forty-five hit him in the right breast, angled left, but didn't come out. Now if one man did it, he'd have to have arms at least fifteen feet long and shoot with 'em both outstretched." He shook his head. "No, two shot him, fired together. Maybe like a pair of gunmen going at the same time?" He looked from one to the other. "Sure, I'll find out who owns the forty-four-forties in this county, but owning ain't proof. A man's got to own and have a reason to kill McLimas."

"I wonder why they didn't unlock the hand-cuffs?" Colley asked. "Strike you as odd, judge? The blacksmith had to cut them, I hear, because they couldn't find the key."

"Lot of answers to be got," Bergerac said. "We'll get 'em. Sign don't blow away if a man knows what to look for. This afternoon I'll get a horse and ride out to where Swigley and McLimas was killed. I'll pick up somethin'."

"It's been a few days," Colley said.

"Now I've read sign six months old," Bergerac said. "Maybe someday I'll teach you if you ain't too smart to learn." He sighed and hitched up his belt. "I guess I'd better get Ed Gruen home to his wife before she gets mad. One thing about taking a drunk home you've got to remember: the wife always blames you, figurin' that you got him that way. You just can't put it over a woman. They got you every time."

Colley grinned. "Not only a lawman, but a philosopher."

"Don't get smart with me," Bergerac warned, but smiled. "And I may call on you from time to time, so don't give me no trouble." Then he winked and walked into Dunfee's, rolling on his bandy legs like a sailor who has been a long time at sea.

Scranton scratched his beard. "It is amazing what we do not see in a man until it is pointed out to us."

"Yes, sir, it sure is. One thing, judge, you may not have the best-read sheriff, but he sure as hell will be remembered as the most colorful."

9

Roan Teal was taken by buckboard to Al Ritchie's place. An owner was supposed to be responsible for the welfare of his paid hands, but Ritchie took the whole thing very badly—Bergerac's appointment and Teal's unlucky incident. The rancher felt somehow disgraced, because an old man had put his knife into Teal before he could clear his gun out of the holster.

He was peckish at suppertime, and his wife, who had learned to put up with his moods by keeping her mouth shut, cleaned the table and watched him leave and didn't bother to ask where he was going.

Al Ritchie wouldn't have told her, anyway.

He got his horse and cut across his land to Sam Mitchell's place; it was almost eight o'clock when he arrived, and he found Mitchell sitting on the porch with his wife. Mitchell's boys were off somewhere, and Ritchie pulled up a chair for himself.

"Didn't expect callers," Mitchell said.

"You hear about our new sheriff?"

"Yes, one of the boys brought word." Mitchell fell silent, and this angered Ritchie.

"Well, don't it make you mad?"

"Can't say as it does," Mitchell admitted. "For

myself I don't care who the sheriff is because I don't run afoul of the law. Never have. Never intend to. Don't know why you should be so riled."

"It's an insult, that old coot wearing a badge!"

"Not to me," Mitchell said.

"Hell, we all know he helped Colley break that farmer out."

"Well, in the light of what's happened since, it was the right thing to do. Colley should have kept on and taken him to Laramie, but I can't blame him for turning back, since he'd killed a man. Bad thing, killing a man. I was forced to take steps like that some twenty years ago, and I'll likely never forget it."

"You know that Colley's got the law in his hip pocket right now," Ritchie said. "Ain't that right?"

Mitchell thought about it and packed his pipe and lit it, and that irritated Ritchie further. "I guess you might say that Colley has influence with Bergerac. But then, he's got influence with a lot of people. The farmers trust him, and so do the cattlemen. I see nothing wrong in it. I know Colley, and he wouldn't abuse his influence."

"You've got some fool notions, Mitchell. Did you know that Bergerac put a knife in one of my men this afternoon? Sunk it clean to the hilt." He puffed his cheeks and rolled a smoke and calmed himself. "There was no call to do that. None at all."

"Hate to disagree on a nice night, Al, but Bergerac never was a man who hunted trouble. He'd make a shambles of it if confronted, but I never heard of him pushing anything." He bent forward and looked closer at Ritchie. "It wouldn't be that he was one of your gunmen, would it? They're a proddy lot, you know."

"Sam, which side are you on?"

"Didn't know we were choosin' up. Explain it to me."

"Glad to. You've got Colley, sitting on the best land and most of it. Never worked for a damned acre of it. And you've got the farmers, squattin' on their acres and sinking wells and cluttering up the waterholes. Colley married into them all right, so they're with him."

"Is that a side?" Mitchell asked.

"Danged right it is. Ain't that enough?"

"What's the other one?"

"Mine. The last of the free range in this whole lick. I don't cater to the law or bow to a Colley, and I'd as soon shoot a farmer as look at one. Now you've got to line up with one or the other, Sam. No two ways about it. Colley and I are going to butt heads, and I'll tell you it'll make the ground tremble and the sky darken. And when it's done I'm going to have me a *big* chunk of range, and my friends will know what it's like to live in all cattle country again."

"And the ones who ain't your friends?"

Ritchie laughed. "Sam, you'll see a big cloud of dust raised, and under that cloud you'll see 'em scattering because it'll be open season on 'em. Clear enough?"

"Oh, yeah. I kind of figured that was the sides all right." He sighed and tapped out his pipe. "You want to be my friend, is that it?"

"I came here, didn't I?"

"I'm not impressed by that," Mitchell said. "You want me to throw my weight against Dan Colley? Al, anyone around here will tell you I don't have any weight. Ol' good-natured Sam they call me. Never quarrel with a man, never look for trouble." He leaned forward in his chair, making it creak. "And I never take sides, Al. Not *for* you or *against* you. Same for Colley."

"I can't let you do that, Sam."

"How you going to make me do what I don't want to do? You say you got trouble with Colley? Man, you've made it yourself. We all know you, Al. It's hard for you to see what another man's got and not want it yourself. But you've got to learn that, friend. There's no other way because you can't stir up anything against a man and not have him fight back."

"I never knew you to fight, Sam. Go with the crowd—ain't that what you've always done?"

Mitchell sighed and clasped his hands firmly on the arms of his chair. "Al, I'm going to give you a free piece of information now, and I hope you learn something from it. Do you remember that surveyor who came through five or six years ago? Not more'n five feet tall, and he didn't weigh a hundred and twenty pounds standin' out in a thunderstorm. Now he was a real gentle man, smilin' all the time. A man might think that he couldn't be riled. But he could. You could start in on him with a bad mouth and he'd fight. Oh, he wouldn't want to, and he'd do a lot to get out of it, but finally, when there was nowhere to go, he'd fight and he'd put up a good one. Get licked for sure because he didn't have the weight, but he'd claw a man up, Al."

"What the hell are you talking about, Sam?"

"I'm sayin' that even a gentle man will rile. So take care now."

Al Ritchie laughed and looked at Mitchell's wife; her fingers skillfully knitted away, and she rocked back and forth. "Ma'am, did you ever see Sam mad?"

"Twice," she said, and didn't look up.

"I'll bet he stomped his feet and swore some, huh?"

"No," she said. "He didn't say a word."

"Didn't say a word, huh?" Ritchie laughed again. "Just gritted his teeth, clenched his fists, and held himself in, huh?"

"Why don't you go home now, Al?" Mitchell suggested. "You've got a charm that wears thin mighty easy, and I'm puttin' it as politely as I can." He held up his hand when Ritchie opened his mouth. "Now I can see that you came here with a burr under your blanket, and I'm takin' that into account. With me meetin' you halfway, I think it's only fair to say good night as pleasantly as possible and let it go at that." He picked up a cane resting by his chair and indicated a triangle hanging nearby. "Was I to give this a couple of good licks, Al, the crew would come running. My way is better."

Ritchie's face was dark when he slowly got up. "Sometime, Sam, I'll catch you on the range."

"I suppose," Mitchell said. "You never could let anything go, Al."

Ritchie hung there for another minute, then wheeled and got on his horse and stormed out of the yard. Mitchell's wife said, "He's a determined man, isn't he? Reminds me of the one near Abilene who was set on calling out Long Hair Charlie Courtwright. My, but he had a nice funeral." Her needles clicked. "Sam, is someone standing down at the far end of the porch? I thought I smelled the lilacs as though someone had disturbed them."

He swiveled around in his chair and said, "Come out of there!"

Three of his men emerged and grinned as they came to the porch steps. Sam Mitchell said, "Smoky, as foreman, you ought to know better than to lurk around."

"Oh, we didn't mean anything, Sam. Al's got a big mouth and—"

"It wasn't going to come to anything," Mitchell said. "But thanks anyway. Good night."

"Good night, Sam—Mrs. Mitchell."

After they walked away, his wife said, "That was thoughtful, wasn't it, Sam? They thought Ritchie would hurt you. But I'm glad you held your temper, Sam. I was proud of you."

"That's all I care about, Anna." He reached out and patted her hand, then refilled and lit his pipe.

Sheriff Louis Bergerac carried his badge in his shirt pocket because he was on the hunt and didn't want to call attention to himself. Moving through country without being seen was no trick at all, and any mountain man who had lived through a season knew how to do it. But you had to know your country and the people who lived there. You had to understand that Indians weren't on the lookout all the time, and even in their camps their guards concentrated only on the terrain at hand.

Hunting parties used to roam this country, but they were nothing to dodge, for they had their mind on game, not on the distant ridges. And it was the same with these cowboys; their work was in the immediate brush, and they didn't have time to be looking around. So when Bergerac made his way south to that place in the road where

McLimas and Swigley had been killed, he did so without being noticed by anyone.

There had been no more rain, and the stage hadn't passed through to mess up the tracks, and Bergerac suspected that the earth pretty well held all the sign that had been left by the killers.

A day of easy riding carried him there, and he picketed his horse and got down and took his time about looking over the sign. Now an Indian scout who didn't know what he was doing but wanted others to think he did would have crawled around on all fours, but Bergerac didn't do that. He climbed onto a high rock overlooking the site and sat there and studied the ground carefully.

He could see where the horses had been shot, and where the teamsters had dragged them clear of the road; there was something of the carcasses left, for the stink was in the air, but he paid no mind at all to that.

It was plain where the stage horses had stood, and equally plain to see that the passengers had helped the driver cut away the harness on the downed horses, because buckles and pieces lay in the road.

Tracks interested Bergerac because tracks told a lot when you knew what you were seeing. He could see where McLimas and Swigley had stood to one side, together because handcuffs had held them, and they were the only two tracks that always remained close to each other. Once they were identified, it was nothing for Bergerac to sort them from the other tracks.

Heavy Tracks got down and helped the driver; that would be a passenger, probably a large man at least six foot. Big Tracks got down on the other side, and this told Bergerac that the stage had been covered by both sides of the road, or the killers wouldn't have allowed a man to get down on the blind side. Big Tracks helped the driver.

The rest had to belong to the killers, and when this was established, he got down and walked around, looking at them carefully. Plain enough he could see the marks left by Mexican rowels that dragged constantly, and he thought of the clanking spurs that Roan Teal and Mitch Dollarhide wore.

Those tracks came from the other side of the road, and Bergerac knew that they had covered that side of the coach. Also he could see where they had stood in relation to McLimas and Swigley, Dollarhide on the far side and Teal over on the other.

Just about right to shoot when McLimas made his last desperate move.

He isolated two other sets of tracks and studied them. Run-Over Heels hadn't done much moving at all, and this made Bergerac wonder what he had been doing. Then he saw something that interested him, and for the first time he squatted for a closer look. It took him a moment to make up his mind that someone had thrown up; the small particles of undigested food convinced him. But it was peculiar, and he remained there a few minutes, trying to isolate what had been bothering him. Then he understood what it was.

That man wore false teeth. He suspected that because no man chewed his food so poorly unless he wore a set of teeth that hurt a little.

Bergerac straightened and wondered who that could be. Not Al Ritchie, who had teeth like a three-year-old mare. It was a puzzler, this fourth man, something Bergerac hadn't counted on. But he filed it away for further thought and went back to study the other tracks.

Pointed Toes hadn't done much moving, either, but Bergerac didn't think that was too important. He knew who belonged to those Kansas City boots. That was one of the advantages of sweeping out a place often; a man looked down at other people's feet.

He left the road then and climbed into the rocks and found where Ritchie and the other man had waited, where they had tied the horses, and where Dollarhide and Teal had waited. It was a beautiful spot for an ambush, all right, and Bergerac found the spent shells that had killed the lead horses. Ritchie had fired one shot and Dollarhide the other.

He got out his tobacco and bit off a chew and thought about it; he believed he pretty well had the picture, but he wasn't sure at all what he was going to do about it. The four of them had committed as cold-blooded a killing as he'd ever heard of, and there was no genuine evidence, not the kind that Judge Scranton would accept.

And it was hell to know who did it and not be able to do anything.

Anything legal, that is.

Bergerac had his own ideas, and he wondered if he could get away with it. Dollarhide and Teal wouldn't scare worth a damn so there was no sense wasting time on them. They were in a dangerous business and one day would try their draw against a faster man and end up dead, so whether they got their punishment immediately was an academic point with Bergerac and one he didn't care to settle.

Ritchie was the leader, but it was Run-Over Heels that intrigued Bergerac. From the evidence, he had done nothing vital, either to stop the stage or to kill McLimas and Swigley. But he had been there, all the way, and he had thrown up in the road.

There were a lot of reasons, Bergerac knew, for a man to throw up, but he suspected that Run-Over Heels was a man who just didn't have a handshaking acquaintance with killing, and it had gotten to him, made him sick.

A weak man, maybe, Bergerac thought. A reluctant man dragged into something he didn't want?

It was worth looking into, he thought, and went back to where he had tied his horse. Find that man and you might find a crack that you could work into a real break. It was hope, all that he had, and he turned his horse and rode back, feeling a little better about all of it now.

10

Before Sheriff McLimas had been killed, Doe Stoddard was considered the most successful lazy man in the county, for he always did enough work to keep his place going and never enough to improve it. His trouble was that he liked to go to town once a week and sit around and play some cards and chew the fat with his cronies and put off until tomorrow all the things that should have been done last week.

But the death of McLimas transformed Stoddard overnight into a stay-at-home, and because he just couldn't lounge around the place and set a bad example for his two sons, he began to work. Paint that he had bought three years before was gotten out, opened, stirred, and the outside of the barn that had always stood bravely bare against the seasons was given three coats.

Stoddard's wife was confused and pleased at this burst of energy, but she said nothing, fearing that if she drew his attention to it he might stop and go back to his old, easy ways. The boys, Ben and Joe, had always been accustomed to doing a lot of work, and now there was more to do, but somehow it seemed less with their father pitching in and getting the sweat up.

After the barn had been painted, Stoddard decided to reset most of the corral posts and sort of line up everything that had been flung together in a hurry in the first place. This work kept Stoddard close to his land and his house, and when it came time to replenish some of the provisions, Doe found himself much too busy to go, so he sent Ben with the wagon.

Stoddard wanted to take some tools and go up to his line shack and rebuild the place, for he had let it go now three years running, and it needed a new roof and chinking and other repairs. His wife, feeling that somehow, after fifty-odd years of careful living, he had finally crossed some hidden river in his mind and had unbalanced himself, urged him to put down his tools and go into town and enjoy himself.

Stoddard was completely deaf to the notion.

Industry and caution dominated him and for a reason he kept to himself. He armed himself with a rifle wherever he went and kept it near while he worked.

So the boys took the wagon to town, and Doe Stoddard took a pack horse into the hills to spend a few days working on the line shack, and Doe's wife and daughter remained at home and wondered where this was leading them. It had been nice to think of having a more industrious man, and it was something safe to complain about, but now that Stoddard had taken this turn, it worried Doe's wife, for he might start com-plaining about the way she kept house or cooked his meals, and she halfway longed for him to slip back into his carefree habits.

Louis Bergerac saw Ben and Joe Stoddard come into town with the wagon, and he watched them pull in behind Dunfee's place, and he went around in back while they were loading.

"Your pa sick?" Bergerac asked.

Ben shook his head. "He's busy on the home place. Suddenly took the notion to work."

"Well, it's been a long time comin'," Bergerac agreed, and went on down the alley.

Man was just an animal when all the culture and nonsense was boiled away; this was Bergerac's opinion, and now here was an animal that had gone and changed his spots, and it made him think that Doe Stoddard had a good reason, one he meant to look into.

Mitchell and the others were acting the same, even Ritchie. But then you wouldn't think that killing a man in his tracks would bother Ritchie, and Bergerac didn't expect it to.

Dollarhide and Ritchie stayed close to each other because they were birds of a feather and they didn't trust each other. They also would distrust the third man, and Bergerac watched them closely, believing they would tip their hand, but they paid attention to no one, and no one bothered them.

And the only man who acted differently was Doe Stoddard, and he broke long established habit to do it.

Bergerac waited for evening, then went to the stable and got his horse and rode out of town and cut across country to Stoddard's place. He would have saved a little time by staying on the road, but he wanted to remain unseen. It was a good night for cross-country riding, with a nice moon and a clear, cloudless sky, and in an hour and a half he topped a ridge and looked down on the lights of Stoddard's cabin across the valley.

Another forty minutes brought him into the yard, and the dog came out, all alarmed and noisy. "Hello, Stoddard!" Bergerac called out and remained mounted. The door opened, and Mrs. Stoddard looked out. She saw who it was and stepped out to the porch.

"Doe ain't here, sheriff. He went up to the line shack this afternoon. Be gone three or four days."

"Well, there's no rush on anything," Bergerac

assured her. "Just thought I'd stop and jaw a spell with him." He smiled and turned his horse. "Sorry I bothered you. Good night."

As he rode from the yard, he looked back; she had closed the door, and he turned south, cutting across Stoddard's pasture. When he reached the other side of the valley, he moved along the foothills until he came to the crudest of roads and took that and rode for twenty minutes, climbing all the time until the valley lay well below and behind him.

In time he reached a high meadow with a creek splitting it, and at the far end a lamp glowed in the single window of the line shack. Bergerac rode part way, then dismounted and went the rest of the way afoot, making no sound at all.

At the window he looked in and found Stoddard busy replacing the chinking in the walls; he pounded with his mallet and iron, pausing only to twist more grass into thick rope.

Bergerac went to the door, slid the bolt quietly, opened the door, and said, "You figure to work all night, Doe?"

Stoddard jumped for his rifle, got it, flung himself around, then stopped and stared at Bergerac. Slowly he let the muzzle drop, and his hand trembled when he put it down.

"You come up awful quiet on a man," Stoddard said nervously.

"Well, it seems you was ready for it." Bergerac

closed the door. "Seen your boys in town. Expected you in, Doe."

"I've been pretty busy," Stoddard said. "Couldn't spare the time. You want some coffee? I can light the fire."

"That sounds good," Bergerac said, and leaned his rifle against the wall. He let Stoddard work at the stove a moment and get the pot over the fire. Then he said, "It bothers you, don't it? Killin' a man." A stiffness went into Stoddard's back, and he didn't turn around or move at all. "There was you and Dollarhide and Al Ritchie. McLimas didn't have a chance, did he? Swigley either. But that poor bastard was done for the minute he put his rope on that calf, wasn't he?"

Bergerac got up and picked up Stoddard's Henry rifle, opened the magazine at the muzzle, and spilled the cartridges on the floor. Then he worked the action to make sure there was nothing in the chamber and put the rifle back.

Stoddard turned around then. "You arrestin' me?"

"Tell me about it?"

Stoddard shook his head. "Louis, I can't. Damn it, I just can't! I don't want to be a dead man. Either by hangin' or Al Ritchie's bullet."

He came back and sat down at the table, and Bergerac saw the misery and the fear in him. "Doe, I know that Dollarhide and Teal killed McLimas. Ritchie was there, and you were there.

116

I could read that much in the tracks. But that's no good in court, Doe. I need a witness, a man who'll raise his right hand and take an oath and tell everything to the judge."

"And how long would I live, Louis?"

Bergerac shrugged. "How long are you going to be able to live this way?"

"God, I don't know!" He wiped a hand across his mouth and shook his head.

"You like bein' scared?" Bergerac asked. "You think Ritchie can scare you? Doe, was I to do it, I could have you running to town in three weeks, dyin' to tell everything you know. I spent the first thirty years of my life with Injuns and I could scare you good enough. I could hide and take a piece out of you a little at a time, and when I got through, you wouldn't have nerve enough to go outside to pee." He reached across and suddenly grabbed Doe Stoddard's wrist. "I want Dollarhide and Roan Teal for that killing. I want Al Ritchie for killing Swigley. I want them hung for it, Doe, swung from a scaffold in town." He released Stoddard's wrist. "Did you fire a shot?"

"God, no!"

"Why did you even go in the first place?"

"Because I was afraid," Stoddard snapped. "Haven't you ever been afraid?"

"Sure," Bergerac said. "But it didn't last. You've got to help me, Doe."

"I can't." He shook his head again. "Damn it, I can't. Ritchie's too strong for me. I'd be like Swigley. And what good is that?"

"Now I don't know that answer," Bergerac said softly. "But I'll tell you this: Swigley's death started somethin' in this valley that won't be easily stopped. If nothin' else, it showed people that they got to stay together with the law behind 'em or get picked off." He slowly got up and went to the stove to rescue the coffeepot from boiling over. He brought it back with two cups and poured. "Doe, I want you to stay alive because I want you to tell the judge how McLimas and Swigley were murdered." He held up his hand when Stoddard opened his mouth to protest. "When you do that, Al Ritchie and his bunch won't be in a position to reach you. They'll be in jail, on trial for murder."

"Hell, the town don't even have a jail!"

"It will have," Bergerac said. "I've got a plan, Doe. There ain't enough nerve in Ritchie or the others to stand up to what I've got in mind. I know how to fight them, in a language they'll understand. They rule by fear, and they fall by fear. It's a law of nature, I guess."

"Tell me somethin'—how come you wanted to be sheriff?"

"I didn't want to," Bergerac told him. "But I was needed, Doe. You've got to do what's right. Ain't Dan Colley taught you that yet?"

"He could whip Ritchie to his knees," Stoddard declared. "Why the hell ain't he done it?"

"You want him to fight your fight?"

"I guess you could put it that way."

Bergerac smiled. "Suppose he rode on Ritchie and wiped him out. How long would it be before you began to wonder when he was going to do the same thing to you?"

"I wouldn't think that. Colley ain't that kind."

"He would have proved he was if he rode on Ritchie. Doe, think about that for a while."

Stoddard sighed. "Damn it, why can't things be simple? Does everything have to be so complicated?"

"If you want to make things simple, you come into town with me and tell me what happened, and I'll go out to Ritchie's place with warrants."

"No," Stoddard said flatly. "I ain't going to die for a damned farmer. Hell, I agreed not to bother 'em, but there wasn't a thing said about sticking my neck out that far. Let Colley do it. He married into the tribe."

Bergerac picked up his rifle and stepped to the door. "You sure are proud of yourself, ain't you, Doe? I'll bet you sleep good."

"I sleep poorly, but I wake up in the mornin'!"

"As long as Al Ritchie says so," Bergerac pointed out. "So long, Doe. If I don't see you again, I'll remember you this way. Scared."

"I'm not ashamed! You won't make me ashamed, either!"

He yelled this at Bergerac's back, for the sheriff was walking away, and it was a lie because he was already ashamed and couldn't do anything about it.

Bergerac got his horse and swung up and then cut down the valley to the nearest game trail and worked his way patiently over a series of sharp ridges to Al Ritchie's place. It took him nearly two hours of steady riding, and then he moved around to come down the creek behind Ritchie's house.

Dismounting, Bergerac tied his horse in a grove of trees and went the last half mile afoot, taking his rifle with him. There were no lights showing but this did not surprise Bergerac, for the hour was late; Ritchie had already gone to bed.

Taking his time, Bergerac made a scout of the house and yard. The only light showing was in the cook shack where tomorrow's potatoes were being peeled. Putting his attention on the house, Bergerac figured where Ritchie's bedroom was, west of the kitchen; the window was open a crack to let in the cool night breeze, and the curtains waved casually.

Bergerac moved close to the house, stepping on the hard, bare ground under the eaves where rain had pelted it solid; he would leave no tracks there. When he was by the window, he put his ear close to the wall and could hear Ritchie snoring gently, and then inching slowly, Bergerac looked in.

Ritchie's bed was near the window, in the corner, and Edna, his wife, slept against the wall. A small night stand sat just under the window, and Bergerac reached inside and gently moved the water pitcher over to where it became a target from outside.

Then he retraced his steps, moved away from the house until he was a hundred yards out and squatted down, shouldering his long-barreled Spencer. He could see the moonlight reflecting from the porcelain pitcher, and he eared back the hammer, took his breath, held it, and tightened on the trigger.

The Spencer roared and belched fire, and the pitcher full of water fragmented, dousing Ritchie. There was a yell and an instant commotion, and all hell broke loose in the house as Ritchie leaped out of bed, swore when he cut his feet on the broken pitcher, and because he was frightened.

Immediately men boiled out of the bunkhouse, and Bergerac hurried back to where he had left his horse. By the time he had mounted, every lamp had been lit in the Ritchie house, and Ritchie was yelling and swearing and promising all sorts of deadly insults if they didn't get out there and find that damned bushwhacker pronto!

Very pleased, Louis Bergerac rode back to town.

11

Dan Colley's father had been a strong believer in open range where cattle roamed free and were rounded up spring and fall—massive drives, the combined effort of all the brands. These drives were expensive, dangerous, and often led to bad blood and trouble between brands and Dan Colley had never liked them.

So when he came into ownership of the brand, he fenced and almost everyone thought he was insane, spending nearly ten thousand dollars to put up posts and wire. It was a lot of money, the largest single investment a farmer or cattleman could make, but there were no more roundups, for Colley beef grazed on Colley land, and the neighbor's cattle didn't muddy the waterholes, and it didn't require three hands' full time to chouse them back.

Dan Colley did not send his crew on roundup, and he saved that expense of wages and horses and supplies. And because he could conveniently move cattle about on his own land, he could work with half the crew Al Ritchie had. But where it hurt was in the time saved. Colley had already cut out his beef and driven to market and deposited the money in the bank while the others were still beating the brush and arguing over haired-over brands.

And he did it every year.

Now, in the late summer, he was moving cattle into a holding pasture to be fattened for fall shipment. Late calves would be branded. Cows with calves would be put into another pasture and hand-fed, which produced better beef and brought higher prices when he marketed.

Dan Colley had built his fence to keep in what was his, but to Al Ritchie it had always been something to keep him out; he'd made a fuss about it, but it had never come to trouble, not the kind Ritchie was dishing up now.

Colley was in the west pasture with Scotty; the crew was doing some late branding on some calves that he had earlier decided to sell but now wanted to hold until the fall market. Another day would finish it, and they had been discussing what the crew ought to do next. Colley wanted them to go up to the west camp and put on a new roof; the crew that had wintered out there complained that it had leaked. Scotty wanted to take the drag and rip up some dams the beaver had built, and they were haggling about which should come first when Scotty noticed the riders coming toward them.

He drew Colley's attention to it, and they turned and waited while Al Ritchie and Dollarhide drew near. Roan Teal was with them, and he had his arm in a sling and treated it gingerly.

Ritchie did not dismount; he said, "You came

to my house with a warning, Dan. I'm returning it now."

"Then say something I can understand," Colley said.

Dollarhide was moving his horse about, and Scotty faced him. "Can't you hold that horse still?" He had a pistol thrust into the waistband of his chaps, and his fingers almost touched the butt of it as he hooked his thumb in his pants belt.

"Behave yourself," Ritchie said, glancing at Dollarhide. "Dan, you put a shot through my bedroom window late last night."

"No, I didn't."

"You're the only man who had reason to," Ritchie said. "Don't do it again."

"I told you once," Colley said. "That's enough talk on it." He started to turn away but stopped when Ritchie spoke.

"Don't do that to me! I'm not finished yet." He got down and handed the reins to Roan Teal. Colley turned back, and Al Ritchie came up and pointed his finger at Colley's nose. Work had stopped, and the hands remained quiet and motionless, taking this in. "I'll tell you something, Dan—I'm not afraid to say it. We've got war going between you and me."

"I didn't push for it, Al. But whatever you do, you go ahead and do it and feel sure that it's all right with me. Now get off my place before you get hurt again." He didn't raise hand or voice, and this made it stronger than if he had shouted.

Al Ritchie's manner changed. He said, "Well, someone shot through my window. If it wasn't you, then who was it?"

"I wouldn't know. Couldn't care, either." He looked steadily at Ritchie. "It takes more than a shot to scare you. Just what did happen?"

For a moment Ritchie stood there, pawing his mouth out of shape. "Well, some sneak came up to my open window, moved the water pitcher so he'd have a target, then broke it two feet from my head. Now it wasn't one of those farmers, 'cause they like their damned shotguns."

"That must have been funny as hell," Colley said. "I'll bet you yelled and cussed a blue streak." Then his humor faded. "But you made a mistake coming here, Al. Don't make it again. And I wouldn't bother the farmers with this."

"We'll see," Ritchie declared, and mounted up. "Someone's got to learn that they can't play a joke on me."

"Didn't sound like a joke," Scotty put in.

Dollarhide scowled. "Who asked you?"

"I just thought it was worth mentioning. You disappointed because there's no trouble? You keep your shirt on, friend. It'll come your way."

"You be there when it does," Dollarhide said, and turned his horse. Roan Teal turned with him, then Ritchie, and they rode back the way they had come.

Scotty and Dan Colley looked after them, then Colley said, "I guess somebody really made Al jump last night, and he don't like it."

"Who you think it was?"

Colley laughed. "How the hell do I know? But I hope that wasn't the last of his shells. After supper tonight you take a ride around to the farmers and let them know Ritchie's on the prod. He'll grab the first thing that looks handy, so keep excuses out of his way."

"All right," Scotty said. "What was the shot for, anyway?"

"What do you think? To make him jump. And he has." Colley winked and caught up his horse and rode on back to his house, dismounting in the shade of the porch. Edith was in her rocker, nursing the baby, and some of the worry left her face.

"I don't like it when Ritchie pokes his nose around here," she said, and buttoned her dress. She took the baby in the house and then came back. "I never liked him from the first moment I laid eyes on him. When he and those two gunmen rode through, I thought—" She stopped talking and pointed down the road. "Isn't that Louis Bergerac?"

Colley, sitting on the porch railing, turned and had his look. It was Bergerac, and he was making his unhurried way toward the porch; he waved when he was still a way off, and Edith went into the house to make some coffee.

Bergerac tied up and said, "I met Ritchie and his friends on the road. Teal's healin' nicely, I'm sorry to say. His eyes looked like two hot coals, and he wants to get even." He squinted at Colley and got rid of his tobacco. "He sore about somethin', or was this a social call?"

Dan Colley told him about the bullet through Ritchie's window, and Bergerac was very much interested in Ritchie's reaction. Then Edith came out with the coffee; she had heard enough of the conversation to put it together. "Do you remember the last time someone played a trick on Al? About three years ago at the dance? He got even for that. He always has to get even."

"Well, he's yappin' up the wrong tree here," Colley said. "But it's been quiet since you've been sheriff, Louis. Going to keep it that way?"

"Don't let it fool you," Bergerac said. "Ritchie's just waitin' to see what I'm going to do about McLimas. But I found out who the fourth man was. And I ain't sayin'. Not yet, anyway." He drank his coffee and put the cup aside. "Well, I've got to be goin'. Thought I'd call on Mrs. Swigley and her brood."

Dan Colley was shaking tobacco into a cigarette paper; he stopped and looked questioningly at Bergerac. "Does that mean somethin' special?"

"I know you made a promise to Ritchie, and I'd hate to see you have to keep it." He pawed a hand across his face and shook his head, as a man will when he's backed himself into a corner and wants a way out. "Dan, I wouldn't confess this to another soul, and I'm holdin' you not to repeat it, but I fired that shot last night. Yeah, I wanted to make Ritchie jump, and I'm going to keep him jumping until he jumps without thinking—then I'm goin' to charge him with murder. I wanted him proddy, but I guess I didn't think that he might look to the farmers after he got no answer from you."

"And Swigley's got a boy old enough to shoot," Colley said. "You fool, Louis! He may ride on them!"

"That possibility struck me," Bergerac admitted. "That's why I'd better get over there."

"We both ought to go," Colley said. "I told Scotty to make the rounds of the farmers and warn 'em. He hasn't left yet, and he can come along. You think three is enough?"

"Yep. Inside and ready for trouble I'd say it was." He grinned. "I know you'd ride Ritchie down if he burned the Swigleys' again. You said that in front of witnesses, and no one can recollect you goin' back on your word."

"I'll get my rifle. You go find Scotty at the barn," Colley said, and went into the house. He had a Henry repeating rifle in the closet, but he took his Spencer carbine instead because Bergerac had one and they could share ammunition. He took a leather carrying case containing six tubes

128

of cartridges, ready to slip into the butt magazine, and he took along three more boxes of shells for reloading. When he went out, Scotty and Bergerac had come from the barn, and Scotty had Colley's horse saddled. In Scotty's saddle scabbard there was a Sharps carbine, and he had a cartridge belt of shells draped over the saddle horn.

When Colley kissed his wife, she said, "If you get a chance this time, shoot him."

He frowned, as though wondering whether or not she was serious, and decided that she was. She was a farm girl, long pushed and mauled by cattlemen, and she had no sympathy, no compassion for the Al Ritchies.

"I can't do that," he said softly. "We've talked that all out, Edith."

"You've killed men, Dan."

He sighed as a man will when a distasteful subject is brought up. "I can only say that I was younger and stupid and didn't know any better." He gave her a pat on the shoulder. "I'll be back when I can. Stay in the house or near it."

She nodded, and he went into the saddle, and they turned out together, riding across the valley to a place where two creeks joined. Finally they came to a swale with a grassy hogback, went over this and dropped down into another valley. At his fence they paused to open a gate, then skirted a field where grain bent to a gentle wind. There was a cabin a half mile beyond, and they rode toward it.

Mrs. Swigley was washing clothes over an open fire, and her two young daughters helped her. The boy was working near the barn, and he ran toward the house, giving the alarm; they all went inside and slammed the door. Bergerac said, "I hope that kid don't start blastin' away before he recognizes us."

It was worth thinking about, but they rode on, and finally Mrs. Swigley came out, drying her hands on her apron and looking very much relieved.

"My, but you give us a scare, Mr. Colley. Do get down. Ella, fix some coffee." She swatted the girl across the rump to get her moving quickly. The boy came out, still carrying his shotgun, and he smiled foolishly and set it down.

Bergerac said, "Ma'am, we're of the opinion that Al Ritchie is going to go on the prod again, so if you don't mind, the boy can take our horses out to the grove along the creek and tie them there, and we'll stay a spell until we're sure there'll be no trouble."

She was alarmed again, for her life had been one streak of trouble after another, and there were times when she thought that she just couldn't take any more. Her husband hadn't been much, as men went, but he had provided somehow, and the children had never been so poor they had to go barefoot.

Dan Colley said, "Scotty, get the girl to help you and carry all the water inside that you can. Fill buckets and pans and anything else you can find." He looked at young Swigley. "Boy, you pull down enough hay for the cows to last a couple of days. Feed your chickens and pigs, then come back to the house. How are you fixed for provisions, Mrs. Swigley?"

"Fair to tolerable."

"We can replace what we eat up," Colley said. "Louis, any suggestions?"

Bergerac looked around. "We got a clear field of fire from here to the barn and outbuildings. All within sixty yards. Don't see how they could fire the barn or anything without getting shot." He walked around the cabin, then came back. "Not so good there. Trees within forty yards of the place. And only one window to shoot out of. I guess we can manage, though. We'll board up all the windows, take some planks out of the barn if we have to." Then he turned and went inside, and they followed him. He pointed to several places along the wall. "We can dig out some loopholes there, just high enough for a man to fire out of when he's kneeling. And we'll board the windows on the inside so they can be ripped off if we want 'em off. She'll do, 'cuz I've held worse places."

They all went to work, Scotty and the boy getting the planks from the barn and Colley sawing and nailing them on the inside. He took the saw and made some notches in them, just large enough to get a rifle barrel through, and to save the precious window glass, he took them out of the frame, and the boy carried them to the barn and stored them in the loft.

The oldest girl was fifteen, a bright child who took all the dishes down out of the cupboard and stored them low so that any bullet that happened to hit the soft chinking and passed through wouldn't ruin them.

Water was carried in and stored, and enough wood was stacked to keep a fire going for several days. By nightfall they were ready and shifts had been assigned, Bergerac and Colley taking the first watch. They sat on their floor, their ears near loopholes; it wasn't what a man saw that mattered, but what he heard. Mrs. Swigley and the girls were in the bedroom, and the boy and Scotty were on the floor by the stove, sound asleep.

Then Bergerac said, "You know, he'd be a fool to come here. But he's a fool all right. In his head he's got it built up to where he just believes no one can touch him."

"If he comes in, turns around, and rides out," Colley said, "then we let him go. Agreed?"

"Be a mistake. You'll just have to do it again sometime."

"That's the way I want to do it. Call it putting it

off if you want, but I want to avoid a shoot-out."

"If he turns away, all right," Bergerac conceded. "But if he shoots, just once—" He reached out and tapped Colley on the shoulder. "Those are my terms, understand?"

12

Dan Colley hoped that for once in his life Al Ritchie would curb his wild impulses and his overgrown ambitions, but he knew it was too much to ask. Ritchie was a man who, once set on a course, could not deviate without feeling that he had revealed some hidden weakness for all to see.

And he hated the thought of being weak.

Night settled in; with all its quiet it seemed that the world had paused to rest. Inside the house no one stirred; they were at their places, waiting.

It was midnight, and the girls were asleep, and Mrs. Swigley dozed by the bedroom door. She sat on the floor, her back to the inner wall, with only one lamp on the table, the wick turned down, shedding a feeble light in the room.

Then Bergerac made a small smacking sound with his lips, and they all looked at him; he nodded toward the yard and put his eye to one of the rifle ports. Colley had his look, and for a moment he didn't see anything. Then his eye caught the shadows at the far edge of the yard—

seven or eight mounted men sitting their horses there.

In a moment they came on, slowly, carefully, and there was just enough moonlight to make them out. They split, fanning out as they approached the door, and when they were thirty yards away, Colley motioned for Mrs. Swigley to come over. He whispered in her ear, and she yelled, "That's close enough! There's a shotgun on you!"

Al Ritchie laughed and said, "Lady, what does it take to run you farmers out?" He waved his hand. "Roan, go bust the door down."

Bergerac said, "Wouldn't was I you!"

It stopped them, that male voice. "Who's that?" Ritchie asked quickly. "Who you got in there, woman?"

"This is the sheriff," Bergerac said. "Take your men and get out. You won't get that offer again."

"Well, I'll be goddamned," Al Ritchie said. "Bergerac, why don't you take off that badge? You look damned silly with it, and you ain't goin' to make a sheriff nohow."

"He'll do until we get a better one," Dan Colley said, and watched Ritchie jerk upright.

"You there, Colley? Say, this is turning out to be quite a party, ain't it?"

Scotty looked at Bergerac, then said, "Yeah, and you make nice targets."

They could count, and it shifted the odds for them, making it less of a sure thing, yet whetting their appetite for trouble. With a yell Ritchie flung off his horse, and they scattered around the yard, letting their horses run loose; someone out there flung a shot at the house, and the bullet thumped into the wall.

"My game now," Bergerac said, and sighted his Spencer; he fired and dropped a man who was running toward the barn. The man fell in a sprawl and lay perfectly still, and they all saw that and knew that he was dead.

No one else fired from the house, and Ritchie's men took cover. Two found the wagon convenient, and Ritchie used the well curbing, and Roan Teal stayed with him. Dollarhide and another man went behind the big oak, and for a good ten minutes there was no sound at all.

Then Ritchie said, "You're not so well off, Colley. Try leaving the house."

"We're comfortable here, Al. You try leavin' the yard."

Ritchie could see what Colley meant, for it would take a lucky man who was very fleet of foot to make a dash to the nearest cover out of range of rifle fire from the house.

After thinking it over, Ritchie said, "When I'm not back by dawn, the rest of my crew will show up. You think you can hold off fifty men?"

"There won't be fifty of you reach the house," Colley said. "You've lost one man already, and I haven't even fired a shot yet."

"You kill my man, Bergerac?"

"Yep."

"I'll settle with you for that," Ritchie promised. "Time I'm through, this valley's going to be cleaned out of farmers and Colleys and old bastards that were never any good, anyway."

He was talking too much, Colley realized, and turned his attention over to the two men behind the wagon. They had inched the tongue around and were moving the wagon closer. Colley had no clear shot for the men were too well hidden, so he turned to Scotty and said, "Put some lead low around the rear wheels."

Then he sighted, squeezed off, and emptied his Spencer while Scotty's Sharps boomed away. In the eight rounds fired, one of the men was tagged in the calf of the leg; he yelled and rolled on the ground, and the wagon didn't get any closer to the house.

Colley reloaded, and from one of his boxes of shells Mrs. Swigley reloaded the tube. He said, "Better look in on the girls, and see how the boys are doing."

She crawled away and came back a few minutes later. "Sleepin' like pups. Don't know how they do it. The boys ain't seen a thing in their part of the yard."

Ritchie and his men began shooting then, and no one answered from the house; they sat there and let the bullets pimple the log walls, and once in a while one would hit the soft chinking and come through, whining and smashing against the inside. Bergerac kept looking out his gun port, and finally the shooting stopped.

"That got 'em nowhere," he said.

"Didn't do us any good either," Colley said. He looked around. "Is there an extra shotgun around here?"

"Ike's."

"Buckshot shells?"

Mrs. Swigley got the gun and the shells, and he loaded it and fired both barrels, scattering the charges under the wagon. It drove both men out, and the wounded one painfully crawled over the tailgate and hid inside. The one who had been there with him had left for safer cover.

"Another five hours to dawn," Mrs. Swigley said. "Do you think they'll wait that long?"

"And then some," Bergerac said. "Ritchie's started it, and he's got to finish it or lose his men. They hired on to fight, not run."

It was time to spell off, and Colley and Bergerac dozed there in place, and the night turned quiet again, for both sides were determined to carry out a long siege. This was an omen to Colley, for he understood Ritchie, and if the man had intended to raid, he'd have hit and cut out. But it was more than that now. They were going to stay at it until there was only one side left.

Dawn flushed pink, and Colley woke, for no

particular reason. He looked into the yard, and there had been no change in position. Mrs. Swigley stirred, went in and woke the girls, and got them to building a fire and making breakfast by slapping them on the behind.

They ate in shifts, staying down and close to the wall, and the girls fixed bacon and eggs and thick hotcakes, and there was plenty of coffee.

Even in the boarded-up house, the flavors of cooking carried out into the yard, and Colley knew that it was bothering Ritchie and his men. But any food they carried was in their saddlebags, and the horses had drifted away, and the first man who tried to leave the yard would be cut down and knew it, too.

There would be no fires built out there, for the only wood available was across the yard in a stack by the tack shed, sixty yards of open ground, and one dead man already out there as a reminder.

Mrs. Swigley said, "Bet that coffee smells good to 'em. You want I should offer 'em some?"

"That's a foolish notion," Bergerac said.

"No, wait a minute," Colley said. "You know, that's not a bad idea. Suppose she took out a gallon of coffee and a big plate of hotcakes with blackstrap on 'em. Somebody out there is going to start to wondering just what the hell he's doin' here."

"You think Teal or Dollarhide would—"

Colley cut Bergerac off. "No, but they're the worst of the lot. Ritchie's got a lot of men working for him who like to play it as though they were wild as hell. I don't think they're that bad."

Bergerac looked at Mrs. Swigley. "You want to do this? After all that's happened?"

"I've been hurt, and I got my hates, but not at everybody," she said simply. "You want it done, then I'll do it."

"Let's try it," Colley said, and yelled out: "Hey, Al! You want some breakfast? Mrs. Swigley's goin' to bring out some coffee and pancakes and set 'em in the yard. Any man that wants to come get 'em won't be shot at."

"You think I'll fall for that?" Ritchie yelled back.

"When she comes out," Bergerac said solemnly, "let me mention that any man that shoots a woman has just found the world too small to hide in."

The girls were working at the stove; they poured the batter on the lids and flipped them when the cakes were brown, and made a large stack. The oldest carried the pancakes, and Mrs. Swigley took the coffee and tin cups. Colley opened the door, and they both stepped out as though no one had any intention of harming them. They carried the coffee and pancakes fifteen or twenty yards off the porch, set them down, then turned and started back toward the house.

Then Mrs. Swigley stopped and turned around again, speaking to no one in particular. "Ain't nobody goin' to do anythin' for that poor man in the wagon?"

Before anyone replied, she started walking across the yard, and she climbed up into the wagon. The man there pointed his gun at her and looked at her with pain in his eyes, then he put the gun down. He was a young man, twenty-three or -four, and the calf of his leg was bloody.

Mrs. Swigley said, "Give me a hand here, Sissy. Gentle now when you lift him."

Somehow they got the man out of the wagon and flanked him, laced their hands together behind him and half-carried him toward the house. Colley and the others, watching from inside, half expected Ritchie to start shooting, but the boldness of it held him. And then Mrs. Swigley and her girl and the wounded man were inside, and the door was closed and bolted.

They put him on the floor, and Mrs. Swigley swatted behinds, and blankets and a feather pillow were fetched, and the man was given a cup of coffee. Scotty rolled him a cigarette and gave him a light, then opened the blade of his clasp knife and ripped the pants leg. The bullet had gone through the calf, taking along a goodly chunk of muscle, and the man had lost a lot of blood before the bleeding had stopped.

The oldest girl got soap and water, and Scotty

washed the wound and bound it with a towel torn into strips. At his place along the wall, Bergerac grunted and said, "Hold your fire."

One of Ritchie's men left his cover and walked across the yard, picked up the coffee, poured a cup, and stood there, sipping it.

Ritchie said, "Hey, you sonofabitch, bring that here!"

The man said, "You want some, come and get it." Then he sat down and ate two hotcakes and finished his coffee. Turning his head toward the house, he said, "Hey in there! How's Dewey?"

"He'll be all right," Colley said. "How were the hotcakes?"

"Good," the man said, and grinned.

"Goddamn you, Rudy, you bring that here!" Ritchie yelled.

The man took his time about rolling a cigarette; he wiped the match alight on the seat of his pants. "Ritchie, to hell with you. I quit."

"You don't quit me, Rudy!"

"I already done it," the man said. He spoke to those inside without turning his head. "Hey, in there! I want out. Do I get to leave or not?"

"You think Ritchie's going to let you?" Colley asked.

"Nope," Rudy said. "But to shoot me somebody's got to stick their head out."

"They won't pull it back," Bergerac promised. "You want out, sonny, then you just walk to the porch, go along the side of the house and keep goin'. Don't stop until you hear people talkin' Canadian or Mexican."

"That sounds good to me," Rudy said.

"Damn you, I warned you," Ritchie said. "If he moves, get him, Roan."

"Consider him dead," Teal said, but remained behind the oak.

Rudy smoked his cigarette down to a small stub, then ground it out under his heel. "Lady, thanks for the breakfast. Dewey? You behave yourself now."

Inside, Colley said, "Give me that shotgun! Scotty, Jack, pour it on Teal if he shows himself."

"He'll show," Scotty said, his voice grim. "I know the kind."

Then Rudy turned and took a step, and Roan Teal jumped from behind the tree, his gun level. Colley shot first, pulling both triggers at the same time although he knew the ten-gauge would knock him over. And it did, sending him spinning. Scotty's rifle boomed, and Bergerac fired once; then there was silence, and Colley picked himself up, rubbed his numb shoulder, and shook his head to clear the ringing in his ears.

When he looked out, he saw Roan Teal against the tree, a welter of blood soaking the front of his blue shirt. Bergerac said, "He caught both barrels flush in the chest, Dan. He never got off a shot." Then he sighed and turned from the gun port and bit off a chew of tobacco. "Ritchie's got two left beside himself. Dollarhide would fight anyone, but I don't know about the other man. Either way, those hotcakes and that pot of coffee did more than I reckoned they would."

From his pallet on the floor, Dewey stirred. "Rudy—did he get away?"

"Clean as you please," Scotty said. "Good friend, huh?"

"Brother," the man said, and closed his eyes as though he were terribly tired.

The sun was climbing, and the day promised to be hot. Colley said, "If I'd ever known Ritchie to bluff, I'd say that the rest of his crew wouldn't show."

"They'll show," Bergerac said. "And Ritchie's got some more reasons for stayin'. You've made him look wrong and look small and he can't take that." He chuckled. "I'll bet he wants that coffee and food mighty bad, but his pride won't let him come and get it. And he wouldn't send Dollarhide or the other fella, either. He's in a corner, and he hates it. Tell you the truth now, Colley—if both of you manage to get out of this, you'll have to settle it with him, just the two of you. Ritchie won't be able to sleep until it is."

"I know," Colley said.

"Don't sound disappointed," Bergerac advised. "Some things just have to be. This is one of 'em."

13

Morning found Al Ritchie completely encircling the Swigley homestead; there were a good forty riders about, his crew having arrived because he hadn't returned to his place when he was supposed to.

Reinforced by a full crew, Al Ritchie found that he could pull out of the yard by laying down a withering rifle fire. Those inside the cabin hugged the floor while random bullets zipped through the chinking, and when it grew quiet and they dared look out, Ritchie and Dollarhide were out of range.

Around noon he sent some of his crew back for the chuckwagon and the cook, and by mid-afternoon they had a place set up, with tents pitched and hot coffee on the fire.

Bergerac said, "That complicates things some. They're settlin' down to stay."

"Looks like," Colley said.

"Goin' to have a little change in strategy here," Bergerac said. "With all the help, Ritchie will end the waiting. Odds are that he'll try an all-out assault on the place before sundown."

"He'll lose some men."

Bergerac laughed. "Hell, he's got 'em to lose. We'll get cut up a bit, too, friend. You notice how many bullets came through the chinking? Accidents, sure, but you fire two hundred rounds, and you'll have twenty or thirty accidents. Some of us'll get tagged. In the cards." He turned and looked at Mrs. Swigley. "Ma'am, I'd like to take every solid piece of furniture you got—chests, tables, bed rails—and bust it up and nail it along the wall to give us some protection while we're down on the floor. Hate to wreck your goods this way, but if we're all dead, a bedstead won't be much use to us."

"You do what you want, sheriff," she said.

Bergerac got the boys to help him, and they knocked apart all the heavy pieces and nailed them to the walls, hammering for well over an hour. Outside, Ritchie was gathering his forces for a dismounted rush, and they came on the run, shooting as they closed the distance. Bergerac, who had the rifle with the longest reach, fired once and dropped a man. Then Scotty and Dan Colley began shooting, and the cabin grew close with powder smoke, and Ritchie's men broke off, leaving four down, one of whom crawled painfully out of range. Those in the house let him go.

"He'll think twice before he does that again," Bergerac said, and looked over Colley's way. Colley was rolling Scotty over, and Bergerac saw the blood and Colley's face when he looked around.

"If someone will fetch a blanket," Colley said, "I'll cover him."

One of the Swigley girls brought one, and he laid it out neatly over Scotty, covering his face and body and letting his feet stick out.

Dewey, the wounded man they had picked out of the wagon, dragged himself over and put his hand on Scotty's rifle. "I can use that," he said.

Dan Colley studied him a moment. "You sure you want to change sides?"

"I'm sure." He waited for Colley's decision.

"If that's what you want." Colley motioned for the man to take Scotty's rifle and ammunition.

Late in the afternoon Al Ritchie, unarmed, walked across the yard with his hands up. He stopped a good rifle shot away and said, "Hey, Colley! You still alive in there?"

"Everything's fine. What do you want?"

"Why don't you come on out of there and give up? There's no sense to this."

"Hell, I always told you that. Go on home, Al. Take your men with you."

"Not until I do what I set out to do. I'm letting you and Bergerac out. What more do you want?"

"Forget it," Colley told him. "You're losing men. We're not."

Al Ritchie shrugged. "Suit yourself. I won't offer this again. How about some of my men coming in and taking these dead men out of here for Christian burial?"

"Go ahead. But where are you going to find a Christian to bury them?"

Ritchie laughed and turned, motioning for a dozen men to come forward; they did so gingerly, as though they wanted to waste no time getting out of there. The dead men were carried to Ritchie's camp, and quiet fell over the yard, and the sun started to hide for the night.

Mrs. Swigley and the girls cooked supper; everyone ate at their stations along the walls.

"Comes full dark," Bergerac said, "they'll come in on their bellies. They won't be good at it, but they'll get closer than ever before." He looked at the door. "That won't take much. A couple of lunges with a timber and it'll be down. After the shootin' starts, they'll try to send in four men mounted with a pole to throw like a spear against the door. Ma'am, you and the girls stay on that far side. Was they to succeed, that door's goin' to come down with one hell of a crash, and the pole will land inside."

Mrs. Swigley asked, "Sheriff, can we last till mornin'?"

"Figured on it. You want to give the place up?"

"I'd rather die in it," she said, ending the subject.

Sam Mitchell came over to Doe Stoddard's place just as Stoddard was sitting down to his noon meal, and in the friendly tradition of the range, Mitchell was invited to join him.

"I don't often see you about at midday," Stoddard said.

"Don't often have reason," Mitchell said. Then he added slowly, "Al Ritchie's got the sheriff and Dan Colley holed up at the Swigley place. His whole crew's over there trying to smoke 'em out."

"The hell you say!"

"It's a fact," Mitchell said. "Ritchie's made his bid. If he carries this off, there won't be any courts or law in this neck of the woods. And you and I will be fighting to hold what we have."

"How'd you find this out?"

"A man named Rudy came through my place afoot. He'd been working for Ritchie, and his brother had been shot. Seems that Rudy got away after Mrs. Swigley and her girls took the brother into the house."

Mrs. Stoddard, who normally kept her nose out of man talk, said, "Why, that was a Christian thing to do, wasn't it?"

Mitchell looked at her and nodded. "Rudy thought so. I gave him a horse, and he's heading for Cheyenne to bring back the judge and the U.S. marshal." He looked from Stoddard to the boys, then back. "Doe, I'm riding over to the Swigleys' and see if I can't talk some sense into Al. You want to come along?"

"Seems I oughtn't mix in this."

"Man, you're already mixed in it. If Al does Colley and Bergerac in, who'll stop him? I tell you it may cost us a lot less now than it will later."

He sat there, waiting while Stoddard thought it over. "I like to mind my own business," Stoddard said finally.

"Doe, I know you're no fighting man, but damn it, you're either with Ritchie or against him. Now you've got to decide."

"Nothing's that clear-cut, Sam."

"The hell it ain't." He glanced at Mrs. Stoddard. "'Scuse my cussin', but I feel pretty strong about this. Don't take your gun, if you feel that'll help any, but come along. We've got to show Ritchie that he's alone in this. He'll get no support from me."

"I guess it wouldn't hurt to go," Stoddard said, his manner reluctant. "Fetch the rifles, boys."

His wife put out her hand. "Doe, you don't get mixed up in this, you hear?"

"I was never one to pick a quarrel with any man," Stoddard said, and finished his coffee. He got his coat, and his oldest son brought him his rifle, and then they left the house together. It took a few minutes to get the horses saddled, then they mounted and rode out, cutting across the valley floor.

They had to pass through Dan Colley's range to

get there, and when the ranch house was in distant view, Stoddard said, "Let's cut over that way and see what's goin' on."

He veered his horse before Mitchell could agree or disagree, and an hour later they rode into Colley's yard. It seemed particularly deserted, and only the cook came out to see who it was, and after he saw, he went back inside his kitchen and didn't come out again. One of the farmer women came out of the house, her manner alarmed and nervous.

"Where's everyone?" Mitchell asked.

"Over to the Swigley place," the woman said. "I'm alone here with the baby." She seemed instantly sorry she'd said that because she knew what a dangerous thing it was for a woman to be alone.

"We'd better get over there," Mitchell said, and rode off.

Doe Stoddard had no choice but to follow him. It took nearly an hour and a half of brisk riding to reach the Swigley farm, and as they drew near, they saw the large crowd of people far back, some sitting on sloping ground for a better view. Down near the yard, in the last of the sunshine, Ritchie's men were spread out, circling the place. There were wagons and buggies parked well out of rifle range, and children played—one threw a stick and made his dog fetch it over and over again.

"What the hell is this?" Mitchell asked. Then he saw someone from town that he knew, and they veered over there and sat their horses. "Sharkey, what is this?"

"What the hell's it look like? Folks want to see, that's all."

"This isn't some tent show," Mitchell snapped, and raised himself in the stirrups. Near the grove in the yard he thought he saw Edith Colley and many of Colley's men, and he rode that way, pressing on through until he was inside this knot.

Al Ritchie was there with Dollarhide. "Now I'm not goin' to tell you again, Edith—you stay out of this."

"What's going on?" Mitchell asked, dismounting.

Ritchie cast him a withering glance. "Nothing that's any of your damned business, Sam."

"I'm making it my business. You want to shoot me in front of a lot of people, then you go right ahead." He took Edith Colley by the arm. "What you want here, Edith?"

"My husband's in there, and I want to talk to him."

"Then you go right across the yard and do that," Mitchell said. Before Ritchie could object, he handed the man his rifle, saying, "Here, sonny, you hold this for me." Then he took Edith by the arm, and they walked together toward the cabin door. He could feel her trembling, and he spoke softly. "Now it won't help him any to know that you're scared. He's a good man, and it'll take more than Ritchie to do him in."

They stopped near the porch, and from inside Dan Colley said, "You hadn't ought to be here, Edith."

"Are you all right?"

"Never felt better. Is the baby all right?"

"Yes. Dan, you're not hurt?"

"No, I tell you I'm all right. Sam, is that you?"

"Yes, Dan."

"Take her home, will you, Sam?"

"All right. Your whole crew is here, Dan. Unless this thing gets called off pretty quick, they're liable to take on Ritchie and his crew."

"I don't want that," Colley said quickly, a bit sharply. "Sam, you see Shorty Peters. Tell him he's in charge. Tell him to keep the men out of it. It's the only way."

"Don't make sense to me," Mitchell said. "Hell, they just might be what's needed to—"

"This is bad enough. I don't want the whole valley fighting," Colley said. "Now, Sam, for once in your life do what someone else tells you."

"He's talkin' sense," Bergerac said. "Now get Miz Colley out of here, and let us get on with this."

"Wait a minute," Edith said. Then she raised her voice. "Mrs. Swigley, this is no place for you and the children. Please come with me."

"My home," the woman said. "If I have to die

here, then I'll do it. But I 'preciate your concern."

Sam Mitchell took Edith by the arm and turned her back. He took his rifle from Ritchie and inspected the chamber and magazine as though he suspected that it would be tampered with. Ritchie said, "You get your business settled, Edith?" He laughed. "Dan tell you he was leavin' everything to his widow?"

"I'm not a widow yet," she said, and walked back to where the Colley riders waited.

Shorty Peters stood a full head taller than any other man, and he was their spokesman. "You say the word, Miz Colley, and we'll ride down there and whet Ritchie's plow."

"Dan wants you to stay out of it, Shorty. You're foreman. Make the men behave."

"I guess that's an order and I got to take it, but none of us like it." There was a lot of murmuring, agreeing with that. "But I guess we'll camp here. Don't see any harm in it if we keep out of the way."

This was a concession she would have to make, and she nodded her agreement. Shorty would hold the men in line, but they'd wait, and if Al Ritchie and his crew broke through and fired that cabin, the order wouldn't hold, and Colley's riders would mount up and hit Ritchie hard.

And Edith Colley suspected that Al Ritchie was counting on that.

Darkness came quickly, and Ritchie placed his

men carefully and went around giving orders. An eight-inch pine butt was brought up, suspended on rope between four mounted men, and they backed off three hundred yards, pointed the thing at the cabin, and waited for the signal.

The dismounted men began firing at the cabin, and the darkness was brightened in spots where muzzle flame flashed briefly, and from the cabin there were no answering shots.

"What's the matter with them?" Edith demanded.

Sam Mitchell spoke from nearby. "They wouldn't waste shells. Dan and Bergerac know what they're doing. Tell you the truth, I wouldn't want to be one of the men trying to breach that cabin."

Suddenly the four horsemen started down, thundering across the yard, the pole bobbing and weaving between them. It would have been a risky, precise ride in broad daylight, and darkness hampered them.

Then when they were eighty yards from the door, every gun inside was turned on them. Instantly the lead man went down, and this threw the end of the pole into the dirt, somersaulting it. The tail end caught one man and swept him from the saddle, and another went into a long diving sprawl, a bullet in his chest.

The log, propelled by momentum, bounced and rolled and landed fifteen yards from the cabin, directly across the path of any other horsemen foolish enough to try the same stunt. Two men down, one afoot, and the other riding as though his tail were afire; it was just another thing that had turned on Ritchie, and it angered him. He ordered the shooting to continue, which it did for a half hour, but not one more shot came from the cabin.

Sam Mitchell said, "If I had to make a choice where I'd be, I'd take inside with Bergerac and Dan."

"But they can't get out!" Edith said.

"Yep. Ritchie ain't had any luck gettin' in, either."

14

With a hundred men, Al Ritchie could have stormed across the yard and probably battered down the door of the house and gained entrance that way, but he would have lost a lot of men, and he didn't have a hundred, and there was no likelihood of his getting them.

The house was pock-marked by bullets, and the door was shredded on the outside, but it stood as solidly as ever. An attempt had been made to destroy the chimney by rifle fire and thereby smoke out the besieged, but they only wasted their ammunition, for the chimney was stone and mortar and only chipped a little.

Ritchie had lost men, too many men, and Colley

and Bergerac were unharmed, still strong and full of fight, and it didn't look as though they were suffering from hunger or thirst. The knowledge that he hadn't made a dent in their defenses was an ulcer, eating him constantly. What had started out to be a quick job in the night had drawn out into a three-and-a-half-day battle and he was losing it and he knew it, and all the people perched on the side hills watching knew it. A couple more days of this and Ritchie would have to withdraw his forces and give up. He was like a small boy trying to move a rock; when he failed, he couldn't stand there and beat it in frustration.

His supplies were running low, so he sent four men into town for a wagon load, and he ordered them to bring back a dozen picks and shovels. Better than half a day was wasted while the wagon was gone, and no shots were exchanged because shooting got nowhere, and a man could get tired watching chips fly.

All their water had to be hauled from the creek a mile away, because Bergerac had broken the bucket that had hung from the well windlass. And after Ritchie tried to send a man in on his belly and got him shot for it, he forgot about drawing water from that well.

When the wagon came back, it was late afternoon, and Ritchie organized a pick and shovel party just out of effective rifle range. None of the men liked the feel of these tools, and their manner expressed their feelings, and this made him a little angry.

"Now, Goddammit, there's no way across that yard without getting shot!" he yelled. "So we'll start here and dig a trench toward the house."

One of the men, a practiced gunman, said, "Ritchie, that's near five hundred yards."

"Closer to six," another chimed in.

"So it's far," Ritchie said. "You want Bergerac to get you with that buffalo rifle, then move in. Now dig this trench at least five foot deep. Pile the dirt up on each side. All right, let's get at it! We're goin' to dig all night."

From inside the cabin they could see the men working, swinging their picks, breaking up the ground so that the men with the shovels could clear away the loose earth.

Bergerac said, "That's mighty hard ground, Dan. I guess we can get some sleep now."

"I want to take a look out back," Colley told him, and went into the storeroom where the two boys kept watch. One moved aside from his rifle port, and Colley looked out. The trees began two hundred yards away, and Ritchie's men were there, in the best of cover, waiting for someone to poke his head out. There was no escape out the back, just as there was no crossing the front.

He crawled back to where Bergerac was stretched out on the floor. "They've got us sealed in, Louis."

"Looks like." He raised his head. "Miz Swigley, did Ike dig that well?"

She was resting on a mattress; she raised her head and looked at him. "Yes. He was lucky because the ground was soft near the house, and he got water at thirty feet."

"Thank you, ma'am," Bergerac said, and scratched his beard stubble. "Was they to work in shifts and stay at it, they ought to be a hundred yards closer come dawn. The ditch will protect 'em so they can dig durin' the day, too." He made some calculations. "Figurin' they'll go a little faster when they hit the soft stuff, they ought to be close enough to rush us 'bout this time tomorrow night."

"And that's the one that'll get to us," Colley said softly so Mrs. Swigley wouldn't hear. "A sudden rush across sixty or seventy yards won't give us a chance to stop them. They'll be up against the walls, and we can't get at 'em there."

"You much of a gamblin' man?" Bergerac asked.

"Sure, I'll take a chance. What's on your mind?"

"Just an idea," Bergerac said, "but I don't know enough about it to carry it out."

"That's a damned poor thing to do to a man," Colley complained. "Start somethin' and then don't finish it."

"I was just thinkin' about how nice it would be to have four sticks of Vulcan powder. That ground out there would cave in if it was given a jolt

158

sudden-like. All that diggin' would be for nothin', and that'd make Ritchie's crew mighty disgusted."

Dewey, who lay by the wall further down, said, "Gunpowder would work just as well."

They turned their heads, looked at him, then motioned him over. "You know anything about blastin'?" Bergerac asked.

"Rudy and I did some minin' on the San Carlos some years back. I ain't a stranger to it."

"Then if you had a charge to set, how and where would you set it?"

"First I'd tunnel out; go right on out under the sill log. I'd go out maybe sixty yards, a hole just big enough for a man to crawl through. Then I'd plant a crock of gunpowder in the butt end of the wall with some cartridges stuck in it. We did without fuse that way. A candle lined up with the cartridges—"

"Shoot at the candle!" Bergerac said, smiling. "Best target in the world, a light in darkness. Sights just center naturally on it." He paused. "Take a lot of powder. Have we got the shells to spare?"

"Well, we're not shooting a lot. Save out a handful to reload," Colley said. "We're just about to the end of the rope, Louis. A hundred cartridges wouldn't do us any good if Ritchie and his crew get next to the wall."

"Good point there," Bergerac admitted. "Well, I'm for diggin'."

There were no tools in the house, so they used the skillet and heavy pot lid, and Dewey went to work. He could not stand because of his wound, but it didn't hamper him when he started down through the earth floor.

The dirt was carried to the walls and banked there, and Colley spelled Dewey when he grew tired. The hole in the floor soon became large enough for two men to sit in, and once the direction was established, burrowing under the sill log commenced.

To keep going straight, a broom handle was lashed to the mop handle, and this was laid in the center of the tunnel so that a man could sight backward; as long as it remained in the center and parallel to the sides, he was going straight. To maintain level digging, an old bottle was filled half full of water, corked, and laid on its side, and served as a fairly accurate level.

In three hours they were fifteen feet outside the cabin wall, for the ground was soft, easily dug, yet moist enough to where there was no danger of it caving in. Dirt was hauled out with a rope tied to a wooden box, dragged in and out, and it was piled around the cabin walls.

They worked through the night, and by morning Colley's hands were raw and bleeding, and the knees and elbows of his clothes were worn through, and Dewey was in worse shape because his leg wound was bleeding a little again. But they were a good fifty feet away from the house—not far enough, but enough to give them hope.

Mrs. Swigley's boys were instructed on how to keep going straight and level and sent into the tunnel. Dewey slept first while Colley and Bergerac dragged box after box of dirt out, dumped it, and watched it being pulled back in. Then Colley had to lie down and rest; he slept on the bare floor, and it was dark again when he woke.

The first thing he noticed was that work on the tunnel had stopped. Bergerac said, "Can't go no farther, Dan. Ground's gettin' wet."

"I think we're about to run into a seep," Dewey said. "If it breaks through, it'll ruin all we've done."

"How far out are you?" Colley asked.

"I guess a good eighty or ninety feet."

Bergerac said, "Ritchie's had his crew diggin' all day long. He's goin' to move in close. Maybe this'll be far enough. How about it, Dewey?"

"Not much choice. We'll just have to increase the charge to give the ground a bigger shake. I don't know as I can explain this, but earth runs in layers. Where we've been diggin', it's kind of firm but porous. But ahead it gets sandy, and I expect that carries water to replenish the well. Farther out, where Ritchie's diggin', the ground's hard and a little rocky in spots. But he's going to be into that sandy stuff, and that's what I figure'll cave in with a good explosion. The force of the explosion will follow these layers."

"Then let's get the charge set," Colley said.

They spent an hour and a half carefully breaking open cartridges and shotgun shells and dumping the black powder into an earthen crock Mrs. Swigley provided. Colley saved seven rounds, a full tube, for his Spencer; the others kept no more than seven rounds, and the rest went into the crock.

The mouth was sealed with beeswax, and three Spencer cartridges, which were rimfire, were imbedded in the wax, mercury bases exposed. Then Colley took the crock and a candle and some matches and crawled into the tunnel after first listening to Dewey explain how the charge should be placed.

He was gone twenty minutes, then he came back and brushed dirt out of his hair and eyes.

"You didn't light the candle, did you?" Dewey asked.

Colley shook his head. "Time for that when Ritchie gets close. I figure sundown." He peered out of a port. Ritchie's progress was clearly marked by the hummocks of dirt along the path of the trench, and Colley knew that these riders hated every foot of it. They hated dirt work, whether it was digging post holes or shoveling around the corral and barn. It was foolish for a man to be so proud that the sight of a shovel turned him to anger, but they were like that, and when this was done, they'd take it out on the farmers. He knew them, and you could always tell when a cowboy had been on post holes for a week; he got drunk and hunted a fight the first thing when he came to town.

Colley's estimate that Ritchie would be close by sundown was accurate enough, and Bergerac crawled down the length of the tunnel and lit the candle. Ritchie had his crew still at it, and Colley watched from a rifle port; they were better than a hundred and fifty yards from the cabin, but that was still too close.

Bergerac had the honor of shooting out the candle; he took a sitting position in the hole in the floor, sighted carefully with his Spencer, and triggered it.

The explosion rocked the cabin and shook most of the chinking out from between the logs. It brought dishes and pans down and raised a ferocious cloud of dust from the tunnel; Bergerac and the two Swigley boys quickly upended the table and covered the hole to confine the dust before it drove them out of the cabin.

Outside, the ground erupted where the charge had been planted, and the ground around it trembled from the wound, and a good eighty yards of Ritchie's trench suddenly caved in, trapping several men in the loose earth.

There was complete pandemonium as men dragged themselves out of the trench and exposed themselves to a clear shot from the cabin. They yelled and ran and left a couple of men trapped, then they ran back to get them out, and Ritchie was there, swearing loudly and wondering what the hell had happened, anyway.

Not a shot was fired from the cabin, although Colley estimated they could have killed a dozen men. Some of the braver ones realized that there would be no shooting, and they dug frantically to free the trapped men. Ritchie got the rest of his crew on the job, and they got the men out and back to his camp.

Bergerac said, "Miz Swigley, it's time for you and the girls to get out of here."

"We ain't goin'," she said. "And I don't want to have to tell you that again."

"Let's get some fresh air in here," Colley said, and got up and opened the front door. The rush of air almost made his head swim; he had forgotten how sweet it was, how cool and refreshing.

It was a full minute before anyone in Ritchie's camp realized that the door was open, for the sun was down and darkness was coming on fast. Then Ritchie yelled, "Do you give up in there?" It sounded foolish when he said it, and a couple of his men laughed.

Colley called back, "Al, you come and get us if you're not too tired from all that digging!" He laughed. "There's a plow in the barn if any of you want to work the west sixty!"

He knew that would sting them; then he saw Dollarhide holding a conference with Ritchie. When it was finished, Ritchie called, "Dan, I've got a proposition for you. Dollarhide wants to kill you."

"He always wanted that."

"Hear me out, Dan! He'll come in alone, and you come out alone. Just between the two of you."

"What good will that do? I can shoot him next month if I have to. Why don't you come in, Al? Bring your crew with you. We can cut you down to pint size, and you know it."

"I'm trying to save lives," Ritchie said. He wasn't getting anywhere, and he knew it. Then Dollarhide said something, and Ritchie reached out to grab him, but he moved too late, and Dollarhide was walking toward the front door, evenly pacing off the distance from Ritchie's camp.

Bergerac said, "Now there's a man just set on gettin' himself killed." He picked up his rifle but stopped when Colley spoke.

"He's no coward, Louis. He can at least have this his way." He turned and picked up his pistol belt and buckled it on, then checked his gun to see if dirt clogged the mechanism.

Dollarhide was walking steadily; he was a

hundred and fifty yards out and coming on, a cool, dangerous man whose pride had been damaged beyond endurance. He had been made to dig like a farmer and run like a frightened man, and he just couldn't take any more of it.

Colley understood this well enough when he stepped outside and stood to one side of the door.

Dollarhide came to within twenty feet and stopped. He said, "It's been a hell of a lot of work, Colley, but I guess it was worth it." Then he laughed softly. "I guess you've got blistered hands, too, so it makes us even."

"No," Colley said. "I'm one up on you, Mitch. You're going to shoot for money, and I'm going to shoot because there's no other way left. So you pick the time."

15

Dollarhide stood there a moment, then said, "What about Bergerac? The minute I drop you, I've got a buffalo slug in me."

"He won't do that," Colley told him. "You're wasting my time, Mitch."

"I don't want to do that," Dollarhide said and drew. He was a good man, well practiced; he drew in a smooth, easy motion, fast and sure of himself, and Dan Colley matched him, stepping to one side as Dollarhide leveled off and shot.

They fired almost together, but Dollarhide had the edge. He had set his target before he moved, and that's where he put his bullet, for once moving, he couldn't change without losing his pace, his smoothness. Only Colley wasn't there, but ten inches to one side, and he hit Dollarhide squarely in the breastbone, staggering him. Dollarhide made an effort to recock his gun, but he was falling, losing his strength, and then he was down in the yard, his legs twitching, his boots stirring the dust.

The men in Ritchie's camp were stunned, shocked to complete silence, and Colley looked up there and yelled, "All right, Al, you're on the run now! Either come in or we'll come for you." He holstered his gun and cupped his hands around his mouth. "Wind River riders! Can you hear me?"

From far off a halloo went up, and someone fired a pistol into the air.

Bergerac said, "Dan, you fool! This place will look like Shiloh!"

"Come along or stay," Colley said. "But hand me my rifle."

"Hell, I'll come," Bergerac said, and stepped outside. Then they all stepped out, the girls, Mrs. Swigley—all of them—and there was enough light left for Ritchie and his men to see this.

Bergerac called out, "Ritchie, you might as well give up. I won't be done with you until I hang you for killing Ike Swigley. And I'm going to get you for it, Ritchie. You and Doe Stoddard. You're the only two left."

For a moment they could see Ritchie standing stock-still. Then he wheeled and headed for the horses. Farther back, Colley's men were getting their horses, mounting up, and they had a straight run down the slope to Ritchie's camp.

Colley was not sure what started it—one man turning, he supposed, one man turning and telling the rest that he'd had more than enough and was getting the hell out. Ritchie was swearing and calling them everything he could think of, but it didn't do any good because they weren't listening to him; they had quit, and by dawn they'd be heading somewhere else, scattering like wind-chased leaves.

Colley said, "No use wasting the effort walking up there. It's over."

"*This* is over," Bergerac said. "We'll have to go after Ritchie now."

The people from town who had been watching this came down from their ringside seats, and Sam Mitchell gave Edith Colley a lift on his horse; she jumped off and threw her arms around Dan and just about knocked him over. There were at least a hundred people around the Swigley cabin, and the fact that they had come to gawk angered Dan Colley. He knew them all by their first names, and he said, "I have a job for you people. In the morning you can help Mrs. Swigley put her place right. Every dish that was broken, every stick of furniture that was ruined, you can replace."

There was a grumble of resentment, and Bergerac said, "The first man that objects has some trouble on his hands. This cabin stands for the homes of every one of you, farmer and cattlemen alike, for if Al Ritchie had taken it, he'd have taken yours, too, when he got a mind to. Now do you all understand that?"

Colley's men were crowding the yard, and Shorty dismounted and came up. Immediately he said, "Where's Scotty?"

Colley motioned with his head. "Get a blanket and take him back to our range for burial."

Sam Mitchell went inside, then came out again. "That place is a shambles. I never seen a place so shot up." He turned as Shorty came out; four men carried Scotty on a blanket, and another helped Dewey. Mitchell said, "Ain't he one of Ritchie's men?"

"He was once," Colley said. "Sam, I'm going to go home and take a bath and eat and sleep. Shorty, you bring Dewey along and send some-one into town for Doc Spence. You comin' along, Louis?"

Someone said, "What about Ritchie?"

"What about him?" Colley asked. "You want to go chase him, then you do it."

"But if he leaves the country—"

"He won't leave," Bergerac said, and went to find their horses, or borrow some, or a wagon—anything just so he didn't have to walk.

He brought up some horses that Ritchie's men had left behind, and they mounted up; Colley lifted his wife and carried her across his lap. Mrs. Swigley and the girls were crying because it was all over, and Sam Mitchell said, "Dan, I'll see that everything is taken care of here."

"All right, Sam."

"If you can, send a man to Stoddard's. He came over with me, but didn't stay. Now the damned man can do something to help!"

Colley's men had already reached the ranch when he pulled in and set his wife down by the porch. A couple of men trotted over and took care of the horses, and Bergerac went to the horse trough and sat down in it, letting the water come up to his neck. "If someone'll bring me a bar of soap," he said, "I may spend the rest of the night here."

Edith had to go nurse the baby; she had been riding back and forth between the home place and Swigley's. The woman who had been staying there fixed a meal while Colley lounged in the wash tub and shaved. Clean, in clean clothes, and his cheeks bladed bare, he felt some better, although the welts and blisters and scraped places left from digging smarted considerably.

The woman's name was Mrs. Kinsey, and she and her husband farmed a section east of Sam Mitchell's; she was a pleasant, round woman who knew how to cook a steak and fix potatoes. Bergerac borrowed some clothes from one of the riders and came to the table smelling of soap and whiskey, a pleasant combination.

They were down to the last of the hot rolls and coffee when he finally sighed and said, "Well, I'd better be getting on my way. Ritchie won't keep."

Dan said quietly, "You can't do it alone. I don't want you to, either." He got up to get some smoking tobacco, then came back to the table.

"Right. But I've got to ride over to see Stoddard, and I'd appreciate you comin' with me."

"All right, but it's hard to imagine Doe in on this."

"He wasn't willing," Bergerac said. "But he was scared. Just as he's scared now. When I yelled out to Ritchie about Doe, I made out the man's death warrant. Now I got to see that Ritchie don't put a signature on it. Stoddard's the only one left who can stand up in court and swear that Ritchie killed Swigley."

"Then we'd better not wait until morning," Colley said, and went to fetch his gun.

Edith didn't want him riding off, but she knew this had to be done, so she kept her objections quiet. Colley got two horses from the remuda, and Shorty had them saddled, and a few minutes later they were moving across the valley toward Doe Stoddard's place.

The thought was in Colley's mind that Al Ritchie might stop at Stoddard's on the way home, then he thought not, for Stoddard was a good jog out of the way. Ritchie would likely go home, get what was left of his crew, and go back to Stoddard's before morning. All of which gave Colley and Bergerac a chance to do something.

There was no light showing at the Stoddard place when they rode in, but this was not surprising, since it was late and Stoddard liked to get to bed early.

When they dismounted by the porch, Stoddard said, "There's a rifle pointed your way so be careful."

"It's Colley and Bergerac," Colley said. "Show a light, Doe. We want to come in."

"Too late to socialize. And I don't want to get mixed up with your troubles."

"You've got troubles of your own," Bergerac said. "Ritchie came to see Colley, and I told him I was after him, and you, for Swigley's killing. Now you put on a light and we'll come in."

Stoddard withdrew from the open window, lit the lamp, and opened the door. He was in his underwear, and he had on his boots and hat. "My wife's asleep so keep your voice down." He stared at Bergerac. "You just want to see me killed, don't you? Ritchie won't swallow that lie at all."

"It's no lie, and you know it. Doe, I'll put you under arrest if I have to, but you're goin' to get dressed and come to town with me where I can lock you up for your own safety."

Stoddard looked at Colley. "You come along to help him?"

"Doe, I just can't see you a party to killin' a man, a farmer or anyone else. Why don't you make a clean breast of it? Then Louis can get a warrant issued and arrest Ritchie."

"You think he can be arrested?" Stoddard shook his head and showed his worry. "He's a wild man, I tell you. You give him his way or he loses all sense. He's just set himself up above anyone! I've known men like that. They're right no matter what, and that's all there is to it." He looked at Bergerac. "Yeah, I was there. I was sick, the way it happened. Ritchie shot Swigley after McLimas had been killed. He just up and shot him because he was nothin,' a nobody farmer. It was none of Al's doin', except that he had to make it his doin'."

Colley said, "You'd better get dressed, Doe."

"You think I'll get hung for this, Louis?"

"Don't see how," Bergerac said. "People around here have known you for years, and they'd stick by you. Hell, Doe, many a man has gotten into somethin' he couldn't get out of without help. It's Al Ritchie I want, and I mean to get him."

"Won't take me but a minute to dress," Stoddard

said. "And I won't run away. Got no place to go, I guess."

He left them in the kitchen, and Colley said, "Why is it that the little men like Swigley and Stoddard get hit the hardest?"

"They're the softest," Bergerac said. "But I'll tell you somethin'—when they point their finger in court, it can be just as deadly as a gun."

Doe Stoddard came out of the bedroom and quietly closed the door. "I'm ready," he said. "We'll have to catch up my horse." Then he blew out the light and led the way out, and walking toward the corral, he kept looking around. He said, "It scares a man to think he could get killed in his own yard. There's any dozen places a man could hide and shoot when he damned well felt like it."

"You get your horse," Colley said. "We'll wait here and keep an eye open."

"All right," Stoddard said. Then he hesitated. "I'm doin' the right thing, ain't I, Dan? I want to do what's right." He waited for an answer, affirmation, something to wipe away his fear, lend him some strength, but he was on his own now and would have to make the best of it. "I'll get my horse," he said, and went into the corral.

16

The town was quiet when Colley rode in with Bergerac and Stoddard; he expected it to be quiet, for they were in the small hours of the morning and everyone was asleep. On the east edge of town there was a large encampment of farm wagons, and the cook fire had gone out, and they all lay huddled in their blankets, a circle around the dead fire.

Bergerac and Colley looked at each other but said nothing; they rode on in and stopped at the express office. Bergerac slid wearily off his horse and said, "I'll go find Ed Gruen and the stage agent." Then he waddled off, and Colley got down and rubbed the stiffness out of his back and legs. Doe Stoddard sat down on the edge of the boardwalk and bit off a chew of tobacco.

Finally he said, "It does give a man pause to think that a farmer woman you never even noticed before could show you what guts really is. It makes you think that maybe there was somethin' in her man, somethin' we missed. A woman like that—well, she's some woman."

"Those kids of hers will do, too," Colley said. "Doe, the trouble with lookin' down on people is that you never really see anything." He went on talking while he rolled a cigarette. "When I came back to the valley, I saw that the farmers were moving in, and I didn't like it any. But I had to ask myself honestly what I could do about it. I knew you and Sam Mitchell wouldn't do anything; it ain't your nature to push people. Ritchie's been a mean bastard since he was a kid, but I didn't think he'd go it alone. I was wrong there, wasn't I?"

"Everyone looks up to you, Dan, just like they did your pa."

Bergerac came back with Ed Gruen and the express agent, and neither of them thought much of getting up in the middle of the night. "I'll be glad when this damned town builds a jail," the express agent complained, sorting out his keys. "Every time you want to lock someone up, I've got to move stuff out of the back room into my office. A damned annoyance, that's what it is." He flung open the door. "All right, help yourself. I'll move the stuff in the mornin'. Now good night!"

"Jolly fella there," Bergerac said. "All right, Doe, in you go. Ed will be on duty right outside." He closed the door and motioned for Ed Gruen to take his position with the sawed-off shotgun. "Tomorrow mornin' I'll send someone to Laramie for the judge."

"No need for that," Gruen said with a superior tone. "He came into town this afternoon with a U.S. marshal. You won't be actin' so high and mighty now, Bergerac."

"How come he showed up?" Colley asked.

"Some cowboy rode south and fetched him, I hear."

"Rudy," Bergerac said. "Well, I ain't surprised. He was a pretty calm fella at that. Teal scared him, but not so bad as to make him do somethin' dumb." He rubbed the back of his neck and laughed. "This does make it simpler. I won't worry so much about keepin' Doe alive 'cause I'll have my warrant by nine o'clock." He slapped Dan Colley across the stomach. "Let's go bed down in the stable?"

"I kind of thought I'd sit here and doze," Colley said. "Two's better than one, Louis."

"Well, you suit yourself." He looked at Gruen. "What's the farmers doin' camped east of town?"

"They're set for war. Barney Fine is leadin' 'em, and he says that if Ritchie ain't brought in, they'll hunt him down. I guess they figure that if the Swigley woman had guts enough to make a fight of it, then they can, too."

"I'll have to break that up come mornin'," Bergerac said, and went on down the street toward the stable.

Colley sat down and leaned against the building, feeling as though he had no strength left in him. He'd gone without a steady, uninterrupted sleep for so long that he could not recall what it felt like. His eyes felt heavy, as though the lids were weighted, yet his mind was alert and kept blocking out sleep.

It came upon him gently, and he didn't know that he had slept at all until someone nudged him with the toe of a boot. Then Colley opened his eyes and saw a tall man standing there; it was barely dawn, and a gray light was seeping into the town.

"Who are you?" the man asked, parting his vest to expose his badge.

"Dan Colley." He got up. "You're the marshal from Laramie."

"George Sutro." He nodded toward the open door. "Maybe you can explain this?"

Colley hadn't seen the door, and he swore and started toward it, but Sutro flung out his arm and blocked him. "Hold on. He's dead. Hung himself sometime durin' the night."

"Stoddard?" He batted the marshal's arm aside and went in. Doe was dangling, his feet a few inches off the floor. The rope had been tied to one of the bars on the high back window, and there was an overturned box nearby, as though Stoddard had stood on this, fastened the noose around his neck, and jumped. There was a large lump on his forehead, and the skin was broken, and it had bled considerably.

Colley said, "Damn it, can't you see that someone hung him? They hit him first, then strung him up."

"While you slept outside?" He smiled and shook his head. "I figure he hit his head against the window ledge as he was thrashin' around." He took Colley by the arm. "Mister, no one could have slept through the racket that was made. I'm going to have to hold you until I get to the bottom of this."

"Hell, I haven't had a decent sleep for four days!" He could see that the marshal didn't care about this; the man was methodical, and he took things one at a time. The urge to haul off and knock this man down and run for it came to Colley, but he squashed it; that would accomplish nothing and surely land him in jail.

"Where the hell was Ed Gruen?" Colley asked.

"Don't know him."

"The deputy sheriff who was on guard!"

"You were alone, friend," Sutro said. He got Colley by the arm again and took him outside. Louis Bergerac was waddling down the street, and the marshal stopped until Bergerac came up.

"What's goin' on here?" Bergerac asked. "You the marshal? I'm the sheriff." He nodded toward Colley. "You got him by the arm for somethin'?"

"Doe's dead," Colley said. "Hung. Gruen's gone. I was asleep, and I never heard a damned thing, Louis."

"Where is Gruen?" Bergerac wanted to know.

"Gone, that's all," Colley said. "Will you tell him to get his damned hand off my arm?"

"You've got the wrong pig by the ear there," Bergerac said. He went inside the express office and stayed a few minutes, then came out, his expression sad. "I take the responsibility for this, marshal. I took him in for protective custody. He was the only witness against Al Ritchie." His glance came over to Colley. "Doe never hung himself. He liked living, even when it was bad." He pawed his mouth out of shape and looked to the top of the buildings as the sun showed red. "I'll give you one guess as to who did this, Dan."

"I know. Ritchie." He made a tight face. "It really must have hurt to have passed me up and let me go on sleeping. But I guess he knew how I'd take it."

Marshal Sutro said, "This the same man who had you bottled up in that farmer's cabin? Looks like he kind of gets his way around here, don't it?"

"He won't for long," Bergerac said.

"If that man was your only witness, the judge would have no choice but to deny you a warrant," Sutro said. "At least on the Swigley murder. You'd have a time pinning down who shot who at the cabin." He jammed his hands in his pockets. "That man have a family?"

Bergerac nodded. "A wife, two sons, and a daughter. Dan, you want to help me cut him down? Marshal, you could get Doc Spence. He lives up that side street; there's a shingle out; you can't miss it."

"All right," Sutro said, and walked on down the street.

As soon as the marshal pulled out of earshot, Bergerac said, "I want you to get out of town, Dan. The minute those farmers hear about this, they'll turn to you as their leader. I don't want you in a position to have to turn them down. As it is, it's going to take all my persuasion to get them to go home, and they might do that if you wasn't around."

"That makes sense. I'll go see Stoddard's wife, but I don't know how she can take this." He turned to his horse and mounted. Then he said, "I wonder how my wife will take it when some-one rides out and tells her—"

"That kind of talk's goin' to get you nowhere," Bergerac said. "Go on, clear out before the town wakes up."

He rode slowly, for there was no hurry now, and he stopped at his own place for breakfast and told Edith what had happened. And telling it made it seem all the more wasteful and useless, and if Stoddard's wife wanted to blame the law for Doe's death, Colley didn't figure he had much of an argument, because there would always be the question of whether or not a man was safer at home.

The mystery of what had happened to Ed Gruen would be looked into by Bergerac and the marshal, and Colley didn't concern himself with it, although he felt like tacking Gruen's hide on the fence for running off. The damned old fool probably went home and crawled in his bed.

Colley had ridden over to Doe Stoddard's place many times and didn't think it was very far, but this time the distance seemed shorter. The two boys were working in the corral, and they came over the fence as he dismounted by the well. They were smiling when he came up, but there was that cast to his face, that expression in his eyes that made their smiles fade.

"Come on into the house, boys."

Mrs. Stoddard was cleaning the kitchen; she stopped work when he came in with the boys, and she knew that something was wrong. She sat at the kitchen table while he told her, speaking sparingly, for there is little one can say except the fearful truth. He expected her to cry, and he thought she would, for her eyes got red-rimmed and the corners of her mouth took on small pinched lines.

Then she said, "Doe—he just wasn't a very brave man, but he was good to me and the children. It would please me if you'd handle the affair of the funeral, Dan. Maybe day after tomorrow."

"Sure, I'll take care of everything."

"If you can find someone who knows 'Rock of Ages' and can sing it, I know Doe would apprec—" She snapped, because everything must break when subjected to unbearable weight.

Colley glanced at the boys and shook his head and turned and went out. As he started to get on his horse, he saw Bergerac and the marshal riding into the yard, and he finished mounting and turned to meet them.

They stopped, and he stopped between them. George Sutro said, "Mr. Colley, we found Ed Gruen at home. He seemed very surprised to see us."

"I sure as hell bet he was," Colley said.

Sutro didn't smile. "Colley, Ed Gruen swears up and down that you told him to go on home and go to bed, that you'd take the watch because you weren't a bit tired. Ed says he argued with you, but you got pretty ornery about it, so he left to avoid trouble."

"He's lying! I never even spoke to him after Louis left us." He looked at Bergerac. "For God's sake, you don't believe him, do you?"

"Nope. But it's your word against his; the marshal pointed that out to me. So I think you'd better come back to town, Dan. Doc Spence is doin' some kind of thing, some examination of Stoddard, and he says he can tell whether Doe died from hangin' or the lump on the head. As far's the law's concerned, we're not positive Doe was killed by anyone."

"Is there any doubt in your mind, Louis?"

Sutro said, "What a lawman thinks and what he

can prove are often two different things. So if you won't give me any trouble, I'll let you keep your gun, seein's how you're not actually under arrest. But you give me trouble and I'll take it away from you."

"Hell, I'm not going to give you any trouble," Colley said, and swung out and around to head back with them.

Bergerac said, "And it won't do you any good to think you can wring Gruen's neck and get the truth out of him. He's as stubborn as a mule, and he's got good reason to say what he said. It makes me look bad, and that's what he wants."

"I've got a right to see him when we get to town," Colley said.

"Yes, that's so," Sutro said. "He can say it to your face."

"If he has the guts," Colley said, and settled down with his seething anger. He kept silent and thought about Gruen; the man was still sore because he hadn't been appointed sheriff, and he surely knew that it was Colley's recommendation that had swayed the judge in the first place. Looking at it that way, Gruen saw his chance and took it.

Yet this bothered Colley, and then it came to him, hit him like a dash of cold water. Gruen didn't see any chance at all. How could he know that the prisoner would be dead come morning? Just going home wouldn't prove anything if

Stoddard was meant to live through the night. In fact, that would look bad for him, deserting his duty.

That meant that Gruen had been sitting there while Colley slept, and Al Ritchie had come along, probably afoot so as not to make any noise, and he had talked to Gruen, or Gruen had just up and walked away. Either way, Gruen had left knowing full well that Doe Stoddard was going to be killed.

Colley looked at Louis Bergerac and knew that the old hunter had been studying his changing expression. When Colley opened his mouth, Bergerac said, "Yeah, I know. I figured that out, too."

Marshal Sutro, who had been riding a pace ahead, looked back. "Do you two know something I don't know?"

"Colley's just figured out his ace to play, marshal. I think he can break Ed Gruen's story." He laughed and thumped Colley on the arm. "You know what that does, boy? It puts Al Ritchie there, right where we want him. In town and by the express office. Now if the doc says that Doe was dead when he was strung up—"

"I don't think you'll be that lucky," Sutro said calmly. "I'm no doctor, but I know that a dead man wouldn't bleed from a head wound like that. I think the doctor will find that Stoddard was alive when he was hung." He took out a cigar and lit it, rotating it so that the flame got to the tobacco evenly. "This fellow Ritchie is very much like a case I worked on two years ago in Colorado Territory. A bald-faced attempt to take over everything—mines, stamp mills, ore wagons, the whole caboodle. He wasn't averse to shooting the opposition, although he poisoned one."

"Did he take over the town?" Colley asked.

"Yes," Sutro said. "We never did prove anything."

17

As Bergerac had said, Ed Gruen was stubborn and stuck to his story, and he proved to Dan Colley that he could lie to a man's face without batting an eye. Marshal Sutro didn't see any point in carrying it further, and he let Gruen go and advised Dan Colley not to push the issue.

Doc Spence took the funeral arrangements off Colley's hands, and he found a farmer's wife who knew the hymn Stoddard had liked so well. The farmers were still talking vendetta, but it was talk now, blowing off steam, and there was no danger, for they were not organized and Colley wasn't about to volunteer to lead them.

He put up at the hotel because he wanted to attend Stoddard's funeral. Mrs. Stoddard and her family came in early and put up at the hotel, too.

Colley and Bergerac ate their noon meal at Dunfee's, then went to the hotel porch to sit until two o'clock. Neither was inclined to talk, and they smoked and watched the people in town.

Stoddard was buried in the small cemetery near the north edge of town, and a lay preacher read a good service. Quite a few of Doe Stoddard's friends were there, including Sam Mitchell and his family. After the ceremony, when Colley was ready to leave, Sam Mitchell came over with an envelope in his hand.

"Sorry to bother you, Dan, but Doe wrote this some time before he died and put it in his bureau drawer. His wife found it, and since it was addressed to you, she asked me to give it to you."

"Thanks, Sam. If there's anything I can do—"

"Yes, of course." He turned and walked away.

Colley went over to a tree and leaned against it and opened the envelope.

Friend Dan:

I always knew you to be a man who never picked at a man's weakness or held it against him. That's why I'm confessing to you that I was with Al Ritchie, Roan Teal, and Mitch Dollarhide when Sheriff McLimas and Ike Swigley was murdered. Lord knows I can't be pardoned. I could have helped maybe, but I just stood there, afraid and sick. For a simple man, whose conscience has always been clear, this is a hell of a burden to bear. . . .

There was considerably more, but Colley was not interested in finishing it; he wanted to find Louis Bergerac and that U.S. marshal and have them read it. He started moving rapidly back toward town, well ahead of the main group of people attending the burying.

Right near the buildings he detected a flicker of movement and checked his stride just as a shot cracked across his path. Colley flattened instantly and rolled quickly into the protection offered by the buildings. His gun was at the hotel, and he didn't waste time regretting old-fashioned respect for a funeral—although, to be honest, he'd never figured Ritchie would be fool enough to come right into town. The man had obviously gone loco.

In the circumstances, Colley wasn't ashamed to duck around the back of the house sheltering him and make his way furtively and silently to the hotel where he found Bergerac and the marshal.

As he dusted himself off, he told them what had happened, and he left them reading the letter while he got his gun. And when he got back downstairs, Marshal Sutro was saying to Bergerac, "Your man's across the street at Dunfee's. Now you can get the warrant first or arrest him and charge him. Six of one kind and half a dozen of another." He unbuttoned his coat and exposed his pistol. "However, as a federal officer, I insist on making the arrest with you." Then he looked hard at Colley. "This one is *not* going to take over the country."

"This is dancin' music," Colley said, "and I'm mighty light on my feet."

"Since you're not a sworn officer of the law, you're out of it." Sutro's voice was flat. "I mean that, Colley. If the law is ever going to mean anything, it can't be continually backed up by well-meaning citizens. Besides, he's already certain-sure gunning for you. He might feel some different about the law."

Then he turned with Bergerac and stepped out while Colley moved to the front window, hoping the marshal was right, at least about Ritchie. Colley had long since been sure the marshal was right about the rest of it—the law had to take care of the law's business, and no matter how well-intentioned he was, a man had to stay out of it as long as the law looked capable of handling its own problems.

Bergerac and Sutro had cut across diagonally to Dunfee's, and they were on the porch now; Sutro was reaching for the door, meaning to go in first. He pushed on the door and opened it, then a gunshot inside was muted by the walls. Sutro clutched his breast, staggered back into

Bergerac and knocked him down. They rolled together, and Sutro's falling weight pushed Bergerac into the hitching post, cracking him smartly on the back of the head.

Colley expected him to get up, but the blow had knocked him out, and Colley just had time to turn and dash for the hotel door before Al Ritchie appeared in Dunfee's doorway, gun in hand.

"All right, Al!" Colley yelled, and started across, drawing his pistol, although it was too far for a fast shot. Ritchie hesitated, then wheeled and ran for the back of Dunfee's place.

Colley stopped to see whether or not Sutro was dead. The marshal was badly wounded, the bullet deep in his shoulder, but he was conscious and trying to sit up. A crowd started to gather, and Colley said, "Help him to Spence's office. Come on. Take hold of him."

One man said, "You ain't goin' to let Ritchie get away, are you?"

"He won't get away," another said, and motioned for them to split, each to cover an end of the street and seal up the town.

Bergerac was moaning and rubbing the back of his head; he could stand with help, and finally staggered to the horse trough, plunged his head under, and came up sputtering. He had a bump started, but he paid no attention to it.

"Where did he go?" he asked of no one in

particular. Then he saw Sutro being helped away. "He ain't dead, is he?"

Colley said, "No. Al ran out the back way. Well, Louis, whatever you say."

"Raise your right hand. Do you, Dan Colley, swear to uphold the laws of this territory? I hereby deputize you." He waved his hand toward the west end of town. "I'll go that way, and you go the other. I want him alive to hang, Dan."

"If he'll have it that way."

"I want you to do it that way," Bergerac said, and got his rifle and trotted away.

Colley ran in the other direction and cut between two buildings in time to come into the alley and head off some of the town people. "Hold on there," he said. "Bergerac deputized me. We'll handle this. There's no use in your gettin' killed."

A man said, "I seen him run into the stable just a minute before you come." He pointed to the large barn and corral near the other end of the alley. "Just the same, we'll seal both roads out of town." He turned and the others went with him, and Colley was alone in the alley for a moment.

Then Bergerac came to the other end, and Colley pointed to the barn, and Bergerac nodded. They moved toward each other, taking as much cover as they could from crates and old barrels and the litter of the alley.

Bergerac was crouched down and pointing up,

and Colley raised his eyes to the loft door, which had been swung open. The snout of a rifle was poking out, and now Colley understood Ritchie's desire to get to the stable; he had had a rifle in the saddle scabbard and wanted it.

Colley tossed a pebble, getting Bergerac's attention. He pointed up to the loft and then at Bergerac, and the old hunter nodded. Colley started to run, ducking from cover to cover, and Ritchie, who couldn't pass up the chance, fired, and the bullet whined off the band of a whiskey barrel.

Instantly, while Ritchie was aiming at Colley, Bergerac raised his rifle and fired. He did not hit Ritchie, but the bullet had come so close to his head that Ritchie pulled back completely out of sight.

Colley came quite close to Bergerac, and the sheriff said, "Al, why don't you throw your gun out and come down? What set you off, Al?"

"I saw you and that marshal cross the street," Ritchie said. "I knew something had happened by the way you walked. A man knows." He stopped talking and waited, then he spoke again, as though the silence bothered him. "What was it, Louis?"

"Stoddard confessed," Bergerac said.

"How could he? He's dead."

"He wrote a letter before he died. His wife gave it to Dan Colley."

Again a moment of silence. "The sonofabitch!"

"You killed him for nothing," Colley said. "Besides, did you really think you could start a war on a widow, burn and kill and get away with it? You've done all the damage you're gonna do. Now come out of there, Al. Your gun first, then you."

"I guess I'd just as soon make a stand of it. What's to lose?"

"You're going to lose, anyway," Bergerac said, motioning for Colley to stay down and work his way around behind.

Colley had no trouble getting to the end of the alley, and he went down far enough to circle without being seen from the barn. It took him ten minutes to get to the rear door, then he leaned against it for a few minutes, listening to Ritchie yell something else at the sheriff.

The door was closed, and the bar was down, but it was an old door, and there was a crack wide enough for Colley to slip his hand through. He carefully lifted the bar and felt it slide out of the hooks. Then the door swung open of its own weight and the bar fell with a clatter.

Somewhere in the loft he heard Al Ritchie move and decided to take a chance; he ducked inside and rolled in a stall just as Ritchie fired down, missing narrowly.

"Now you've got one inside and one out," Colley said from the safety of the stall. "If you want to look out, you'll find that Bergerac's not in the alley. Things are about run out for you, Al. You wanted to ride big, but you're afoot now. It's all over."

"The hell it is!" Ritchie said. "I'll kill me a Colley yet before I'm done."

There was a clatter in the front of the barn as Bergerac rushed in and stumbled over a casually placed oat bucket. He made his cover before Ritchie could get to him.

Colley said, "Now we're both inside, Al. You're not doin' so good." He moved because he was sitting on something uncomfortable, and when he felt down there, he found an old knot that had fallen out of the stall planks. Colley hefted it, then threw it upward, hitting the bottom of the loft.

Ritchie fired from reflex, and Dan Colley laughed.

"Got you pretty jumpy, huh, Al? We're in no hurry. It'll be dark soon, then we can come in crawling, and you'll never now we're there until it's too late. Bergerac can use his knife, like the old days."

"Goddammit! You don't scare me. I'll settle this with you man to man!"

"Can't do that," Colley said. "I've got to arrest you."

"You're a coward!"

"You don't believe that, Al. But Bergerac deputized me, and I don't dare do what I want anymore." He fell silent and remained that way for five minutes, peering out between the gaps in the stall planks.

He saw movement farther down, on the other side, and saw that Bergerac was in another stall there. The loft ladder was very close, and Bergerac was working a hay fork against it, teetering it, trying to knock it down and seal off the loft.

Ritchie tried to stop this by reaching down and grabbing it, but Colley was waiting for this, and he sighted, fired, and nicked Ritchie in the forearm, making him yelp and draw back.

The diversion was enough to make the opportunity Bergerac needed; he toppled the ladder and it came down, raising a cloud of dust and breaking several rungs from it.

"You want to jump down out the loft door," Colley said, "you go ahead, but you'll break a leg. That's thirty feet to the ground." He laughed. "I'd say you're in worse shape than we were in the Swigley place."

Ritchie said nothing, but when he moved, straw and dust sifted down through the cracks in the planks, and they knew where he was. Bergerac shot with his Spencer, and the bullet must have gone through, for Ritchie moved quickly, then all was quiet.

"Now we don't want to kill you, Ritchie," Bergerac said. "You got to stand trial, just like Swigley did. It's the only chance you got."

"Some chance!"

"Better than you gave Swigley," Bergerac said. "Or Doe Stoddard. Be a man about this, Ritchie. You were born to hang, and that'll likely happen. But you'll have your say in court, and maybe you'll be lucky. It's happened before."

"I'd never live to stand trial!"

"You suit yourself," Colley told him. "We can wait. So if you decide to throw down your gun, we'll be here. Make a fight of it, and we'll be here for that, too. This is the one thing you won't run from or shoot your way out of."

"When I don't come home, my wife'll send the whole crew in after me," Ritchie yelled.

"What crew?" Bergerac said. "You take your time, Al. Think it over. We're in no rush. Colley, come suppertime, you want me to hold here while you go eat?"

"Unless you want to go first."

"No, I can wait. You want to bring somethin' back for Al? We can send it up in a bucket."

"Let him get his own."

"Now he ain't exactly in a position to do that," Bergerac said.

"That's tough," Colley said. "But the last time he was offered cakes and coffee he got smart about it and made trouble."

"Why don't you shut up down there? Why don't you go away and leave me alone?"

For a moment Bergerac remained silent, then

he said, "Ritchie, we can both remember the day in this country where we did leave a man alone. We rode wide around him and hoped he'd never come our way. But times have changed. These men have to be put away where they can't hurt people. You're a lobo wolf, Ritchie. Maybe it ain't your fault, but you've got to be put away. I don't guess you understand that, and it don't matter none whether you do or not. But it's a fact. We'll be here when you decide which way it's to be."

18

It was late afternoon, and for nearly two hours neither Colley nor Sheriff Bergerac had moved, and in the loft Al Ritchie was completely quiet. Outside the barn, in the alley, and on the back street, the crowd gathered, forty or so at first, and then it swelled to nearly a hundred men. Colley could look out the back door and see a part of them, standing there, some of them armed, but most of them carrying no weapons at all.

They just stood there and looked at the barn.

Then Judge Scranton called out: "Sheriff, can you hear me? This is Judge Scranton."

"Hear you just dandy, judge."

"Are you pinned down inside there, sheriff?"

Bergerac chuckled. "Well, judge, I don't guess

we could just walk out without gettin' shot at, but we can get out easier than Ritchie can. What's on your mind?"

"I want you to come out of there," Scranton said.

"All right." Bergerac lowered his tone of voice. "You go first, Dan. If he moves overhead to pot you out the back, I'll shoot through the planks with this buffalo gun. Once you get outside, get a rifle and cover the front loft door. I'll run for it, and if he pokes out, blow his head off."

"Any time you're set," Colley told him.

"I'm set."

Colley holstered his pistol, eased out of the stall, and moved carefully toward the open back door, all the time looking upward at the loft for telltale signs of drifting dust. But Ritchie didn't move; he had a healthy respect for Bergerac's buffalo rifle. Colley dashed to the corral fence, vaulted over, and went around to the front.

Dunfee was there, a repeating Henry rifle cradled in the crook of his arm, and Colley took it and watched the front loft door. "All right, Louis, any time!"

Ritchie put the muzzle of his rifle out and Colley rolled off three shots as fast as he could work the lever, splintering the frame of the opening, and Bergerac was in the clear then, and Ritchie didn't get to fire even once.

Judge Scranton eased up, gently moving people

aside, and Bergerac came over, and almost everyone watched the barn. Scranton said, "Sheriff, you'll be pleased to know that Dr. Spence removed the bullet from Marshal Sutro, and he'll be all right. However, that's not what I called you out here for." He looked at the silent, waiting crowd. "I think we have reached one of those rare moments when the masses are united by common bond, by one unspoken thought. I'd like to speak to him, with your permission, sheriff."

"You don't need my permission, judge." Bergerac waved his hand, indicating his agreement.

"Thank you, sheriff. Alfred Ritchie, this is Judge Scranton! Can you hear me in there?"

"Yeah, I hear you."

"The best thing you can do is to throw down your gun and come out of there. Your weapons are quite useless."

Al Ritchie laughed. "Come in and get me."

"That's unnecessary," Scranton said. "Mr. Ritchie, look outside. Look at the people standing there. Do you think you could shoot your way through them? You might succeed in killing a few, but they'd fall on you with their bare hands, and you would never escape."

"There ain't a man out there who has guts enough to stand up against me!"

"If you really believe that, then you should have

no trouble coming down and walking out of there," Scranton said. "But you know that Sheriff Bergerac and Dan Colley will be here. There's no way out for you, Mr. Ritchie. If you stay out the night, then we'll be here in the morning."

Ritchie's voice rose to a wild yell. "Ain't there any men left? What kind of dirty cowards are you that you can't come in and get me?"

This had no effect on the people standing around; it was like the temper tantrum of a child, completely ignored as something that would pass by itself and leave no scar, no residue, no impression of any kind.

Scranton said, "No one has to come in and get you out of there, Mr. Ritchie, because you're already finished. You just want to go through some useless motions." He seemed very determined that Ritchie understand. "We are no longer living in a time or place where each man must settle for himself the troubles that life brings. Sheriff Bergerac does not have to prove to these people that he is a brave man. Or Dan Colley. They know what they are. And they know now what you are, Mr. Ritchie—a man blinded by rage and ambition and inflated opinion of himself. It's led you to this, without one friend in the world. You want to escape. There is no escape from murder and pillage. There is no out, Mr. Ritchie, except down from the loft and out the door and into a courtroom."

"You think I'm dumb enough to walk out and be hung?" He laughed wildly. "Listen, if I had Teal and Dollarhide and Waggoner with me, I'd show you a fight of it. We'd shoot up this damned place all right. By God, we'd thin out the farmers and the weak bastards in a hurry. And we'd get you, Colley! By God, we'd get you for sure!"

"They're all dead, Al," Dan Colley said. "Can't you understand? There's no one but you left. There's just you to hang all by yourself." When he said it, he knew that he had come to the touchstone of it all; Al Ritchie was not afraid of dying, but he didn't want to die alone. It was the responsibility of it that terrified him, the feeling that the others had gotten off easier than he. And Colley remembered all the things Ritchie had ever done, not alone, because he didn't have that kind of conviction. He had dragged Doe Stoddard along because he wanted to spread his guilt to another man. And the night he had gone to town and given Joe Waggoner the rope—it had been the same thing.

This was the man's weakness, his inability to stand alone, and now he was alone, completely, irrevocably, and he couldn't stand to look at it, to admit it.

Colley looked around at the people and saw that they did not hate Al Ritchie any more than they hated drought or insect pests that denuded their crops. The man was the last of a blight, and they were going to see it ended, stamped out.

The sound of the shot was muffled, but it made them all jump. Bergerac frowned and looked at Colley, who said, "Cover me, Louis. I'll go take a look."

And before Bergerac could object, Colley drew his pistol and dashed toward the door. There was no sign of Ritchie, and once Colley got inside Bergerac lowered his rifle.

The sun was going fast, and the barn was filled with gray shadows deep in the backs of the stalls. Colley stopped and listened, but he could hear no movement at all. Yet there was a sound, a slow, steady dripping, and he looked up toward the loft until he found it. Blood dripped from between the cracks, and he left his place by the door, got the loft ladder, erected it, and cautiously went up. He was careful as he put his head and gun over, and he had to turn slightly to see Al Ritchie.

He was slumped against some loose hay, his head canted back, the pistol that had blown off part of his head was loosely held in his hand. Colley crawled over and looked at him, then went to the front loft window. "Louis, send up a couple of men and the doc. Al killed himself."

Immediately everyone turned and started to walk away, and it surprised Colley, the way they did it—instantly, as though he had given them some kind of signal. And he supposed he had done just that, for with Al Ritchie dead the blight was lifted, and they could go to their homes and work their fields and brand their cattle and not have any fear when a stranger appeared, and there would be no fear of one another.

Bergerac and two other men came up the ladder; one of them had a lighted lantern, and he shone it on Ritchie and said, "Somehow you just got to feel sorry for him, don't you?"

Dan Colley left the barn and met Dr. Spence hurrying along. "Have you seen Judge Scranton, doc?"

Spence pointed back toward the main street and rushed on. Colley went to the end of the alley, walked a short distance, then turned to the hotel. Scranton was on the porch, talking quietly to some of the townspeople; they smiled and left as Colley came up.

"I suppose he had a family," Scranton said.

"Yes, there's always someone to cry, judge."

"How true. What will become of them?"

"I guess Sam Mitchell and I can buy them out, and that'll give them something to move on with. It's not likely Ritchie's family will want to stay on around here."

The judge looked carefully at Dan Colley. "Do you mind if I ask you something personal?"

"No, go right ahead."

"Before you came home to manage your legacy, you had quite a reputation as a gunfighter.

But all that was put behind you. May I ask you why?"

Colley rolled a cigarette and considered his answer. "I came to this—not this town; it doesn't matter where—and it was wide open. A man took care of himself, or he left in a hurry for a safer place. As you say, my reputation was well enough established so that I was generally left alone. They walked wide of me. I liked it, being someone, then one day I noticed something. I kept going into this store for my tobacco and shaving soap, and I saw that the clerk was afraid of me. He wasn't a little man, but he *was* a gentle man, and while the town was just right for a man who wore a pistol and could use it, it wasn't just right for him. He lived in terror for he was pestered by everyone with a notion to bully someone. There just wasn't anyone in that town to take care of his rights. He didn't have any, except what was thrown to him from day to day, like bones to stray dogs. Then I started looking around, and there were a lot like him, all scared, all unable to do anything about it. And somehow it didn't feel so good anymore to be a big man." He shrugged. "Then Pa died and I came here. And I stood against Al Ritchie. It's pretty simple, judge."

"Simple?" Scranton laughed softly. "Justice is never simple, Dan." He took out his watch and looked at it, then snapped the lid closed and returned it to his pocket. "Well, it's my bedtime; I've got to catch the stage at six o'clock in the morning." He offered his hand. "I may not see you again, Dan, so I'll leave you with something to think about. Al Ritchie is dead, gone. He wasn't the last of his kind. Ritchie was a growth, so keep an eye on the crops as they sprout."

"Why me?"

"Man, you were born for it. It's part of the legacy." He turned and went inside. Colley watched him a moment and understood that Scranton had been totally right, and there was nothing he could do about it or wanted to do about it.

His horse had been moved from where he had tied it; someone had fed the animal and grained him, and Colley went down the street in search of him. The urge to get home was a driving force now. Edith would light into him for staying so long, and it would be good to have her rag him a little and bang pans in the kitchen and scold him for never being on time for meals and always letting his own affairs go to help someone else. But while she did it, he would know that she loved him and that he was right and that she wouldn't have it any other way.